Trading Spaces ™

BOYS VS. GIRLS

Written by:
Sharon Lennon &
Mona Mansour

Scholastic Inc.

New York   Toronto   London   Auckland   Sydney

Mexico City   New Delhi   Hong Kong   Buenos Aires

The publisher and authors of *Trading Spaces: Boys vs. Girls* wish to acknowledge the following people:

For the cover — Photograph: James Levin/Studio 10 and Brad Miller; Art Director: Joan Moloney; Designer: Peter Koblish; Stylist: Kim Field; Hair and Makeup: Kathy Morano

For the interior — With the exception of the before and after room photographs, all images from Chapter 8 by Laura Pedrick; all other photographs and icons courtesy of the Discovery Channel and Banyan Productions; Art Director: Joan Moloney; Designer: Keirsten Geise; Photo Editor: Sharon Lennon; Design and Craft Consultant: Kerry Lennon; Editorial assistance to the authors: Minju Pak

From Discovery Communications, Inc. and Banyan Productions — Marjorie Kaplan; Karen Stein Solomon; Jim Rapsas; Sharon M. Bennett; Dee Scott; Carol LeBlanc; Erica Green; the fantastic staff at Banyan Productions

ISBN 0-439-60730-2

© 2003 Discovery Communications, Inc.

3 4 5 6 7 8/0

Printed in the U.S.A.
First printing, November 2003

Contents

Introduction

Your Room, Your Way, Your Turn!

Are you too cool for your crib? Too savvy for your space? Too cramped in your cocoon? Need more Zen for your zone? Bored with your bedroom, over it, outgrown it?

Well, congratulations. You've already taken the first step to fixing it.

Here comes the how-to. Flip through the eye-popping pages of this book and get the inside scoop on how to create a room that rocks and reflects today's spankin' new you.

The deal:

TV's *Trading Spaces* debuted in 2000 to insta-success. The concept was awesome. Armed with a posse of professionals — decorators, designers, handymen and handywomen — a budget, and a 48-hour time frame, neighbors get to redo one room in each other's homes. The results range from wide-eyed euphoria to "how could you?" shock. *Trading Spaces* is riveting TV, a must-see for all ages.

Your deal:

In spring 2003, *Trading Spaces: Boys vs. Girls* bounced onto the airwaves. You can catch it on Discovery Kids on NBC Saturday mornings, and also find it on Discovery Kids Channel. Same idea as the original, but with a ticklish twist: A team of two girls gets to renovate the bedroom

Stuff you will NOT need...

1. Lots of money
2. Lots of time
3. Lots of professionals

of a boy — friend or sibling. At the same time, the two guys roll up their sleeves and magically transform a girl's crib.

Your book:

This *Trading Spaces: Boys vs. Girls* book shows how the rooms on TV were redone, but mostly it's about how-you-can-too. We've divided this book into chapters based on themes from the TV show. You'll see how you can copy those rooms, customize them, and/or take just one part — that awesome headboard, supreme wallpaper, rockin' rug — and put your own personal stamp on it.

Use us for inspiration — get ideas, tips, tools, and concrete "let's get real" advice. This is the place to fire up your imagination.

Maybe you're thinking, *But I want to be on TV!* Want in on some of the *Trading Spaces* action firsthand? Here's what you do: Apply. You can find the application online at *www.DiscoveryKids.com*. There will be photos and room measurements to send in, and follow-up interviews by the show's researchers and producers. But as any *Trading Spaces* boy or girl will tell you, it's well worth the effort!

Stuff you WILL need...

1. Parents' OK
2. Imagination
3. Creativity
4. A list of things you like (and don't like!)
5. And most of all... a craving for some F-U-N

Alex

Alex, age 13, is an aspiring actress who likes hot and spicy colors!

Thanks to *Trading Spaces*, Alex can have her Hollywood dream room — if her friend Jeremiah knows her well enough to help design it.

Jena

And does Alex know Jeremiah well enough to redo his room? She's teamed up with friend Jena to give it a try!

Chapter 1

HOLLYWOOD STYLE

Ever think twice about inviting people over because they might take one look at your digs and get the wrong impression of you?

Are your talents and interests reflected in the most important room in the house — your bedroom? If you're anything like the *Trading Spaces: Boys vs. Girls* teammates, the answer is no. No need to freak out. Why not step up to the challenge

A ROOM FOR A STAR

"Alex likes to dance and act. She wants to be in Hollywood someday." — Jeremiah

SKATE PARK

and transform your room and your life? You can do it alone or with a friend.

Jeremiah and Alex traded spaces in the hopes of trading up to a cooler crib. The results were awesome. They knew each other well enough to take out the old and bring in the new, with a total transformation that matched each of their unique personalities.

RADICAL RAMPS & RETRO

"Jeremiah likes snowboarding and skateboarding." — Jena

Jeremiah

Jeremiah, age 12, is into extreme sports and anything retro.

This 'boarder has some serious boredom issues. At least, his bedroom does. It's dark and drab and pretty basic. A triple yawn.

With a little help from buddy Alex, Jeremiah's room is going to get the wake-up call it craves.

Jon

Meanwhile, Jeremiah and his teammate, Jon, will give Alex's room a dramatic new flair!

5

ALEX'S CRIB RE-CREATED!

Star power: Decorator Jordin and the guys rolled out the red carpet so Alex will always feel like she's making an entrance. Even if you wouldn't be caught dead playing Romeo in the school play or tapping in the next dance recital, this room is bound to make you feel like a star. Besides, who doesn't like going to the movies?

You, too, can learn the design tricks Jordin used for Alex's room — everything you need to know is packed right into this chapter.

What's WRONG with This Picture?

Be honest: Is your room just too yesterday? Are you completely over the posters on your wall? Did the stuffed animals arrive on your first birthday and never leave? There's nothing wrong with being sentimental, but if your room reflects the old you — with styles from five years ago — it might be time for an update.

BEFORE

Alex, what's up with all the giraffes?

Where's the pizzazz?

"I want my bedroom to be not as kidlike. I want it to have a lot of pizzazz." — Alex

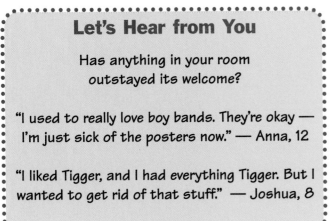

Let's Hear from You

Has anything in your room outstayed its welcome?

"I used to really love boy bands. They're okay — I'm just sick of the posters now." — Anna, 12

"I liked Tigger, and I had everything Tigger. But I wanted to get rid of that stuff." — Joshua, 8

It's up to Alex's friends Jeremiah and Jon to redo her room with flair and star quality. Jordin, designer extraordinaire, knows just how to make it glamorous — Hollywood-style.

Okay, so you're ready for a change. Congratulations! But that doesn't mean you have to get rid of all of the old when you bring in the new. No need for a total overhaul. And if something in your room has a long history of making you happy, don't let anyone tell you it's got to go.

What's RIGHT with This Picture?

Now Alex can sit back and enjoy the show with two old movie theater seats. Thankfully, no nasty gum stuck underneath.

AFTER

Back in the Day: The Red Carpet

Of course, you can watch the Academy Awards to see stars strut on down the red carpet. But get this: The tradition of "rolling out the red carpet" dates as far back as ancient India! Jahangir, the emperor from 1605 to 1627, once paid a visit to his brother-in-law on New Year's Day. To celebrate his arrival, Jahangir's brother-in-law draped the road between his house and the palace with a red velvet carpet so that the royal emperor and his posse would never have to touch the ground.

This handmade sign reminds Alex to get ready for her close-up.

JEREMIAH'S DIGS REDONE!

Bust it out! Jeremiah's room was transformed from a drab and depressing dark blue (sorry, Mom!) to an awesome array of colors. The before-and-after difference? His friends know him as a "wild" guy. Designer Scott, who's also got a bit of a wild streak, helped the girls put their knowledge of Jeremiah to work — and they created a space that is an extension of the real Jeremiah.

Consider THIS

You're ready to go.
Change is in the air. But it's your room, right? So take a minute to figure out what matters most to you. Before you dive in, ask yourself:

In your room, what's most important to you?

a. comfort
b. color and style
c. coolness/funkiness
d. keeping it clean enough to see the floor

BEFORE

"I want my bedroom redone because it's too dark." — Jeremiah

These wooden blocks are probably not what Jeremiah had in mind when he said he liked anything retro.

Alex and Jena, paired up with designer Scott, prepare to launch into high gear with a radical overhaul of Jeremiah's room.

This hoop would be great if you were two feet tall.

Consider THAT

Think you know your room? Think again. Get your best friend to move something in your room from one place to another without telling you. See if you can tell what changed. See if you like it. Sometimes change isn't so bad!

That disco-fever feeling is achieved with a bunch of disco balls that dangle and sparkle, reflecting the wild palette of colors in Jeremiah's revamped room.

The lights on this headboard skating ramp are voice activated!

AFTER

Back in the Day: The Lava Lamp

This groovy light came out in 1963, way before Austin Powers was saying, "Yeah, baby," to movie audiences. Inventor Edward Craven Walker spent 10 years mixing oil and water into bloblike consistencies before creating the first Astro Lamp. Eventually it morphed into the Lava Lamp and became an ultrahip, must-have item in the sixties and seventies.

Peel, Paint & Ponder

How does that *Trading Spaces* team do it?

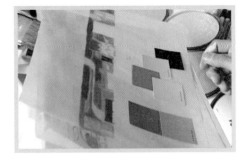

They transformed Jeremiah's and Alex's rooms in two days flat! Are you ready to learn a few tricks of the trade? Let's start with a biggie — the paint job.

Scott pulled a bunch of colors that are extreme and in line with Jeremiah's tastes. He looked at the colors that Jeremiah surrounds himself with, from snowboards to his tie-dyed T-shirts. Then he and the girls came up with a pattern to paint the colors on Jeremiah's wall.

Color is key: One of the most important parts of a theme is color.

Bye-bye, giraffes. The boys slap the first coat of gold paint on the walls of Alex's room. A bold choice — but it works for Alex. And gold just happens to be the same color as the award statuettes at the Oscars.

Dude, where's my color?

What colors are you most attracted to? Not sure how to answer this question?

Try this: Pour out a big box of crayons (the more the better). Pick out the three colors that you're most into. Try matching them up to see what they look like together.

Room redos are much easier when they are a team effort. So why not try . . .

THE BUDDY SYSTEM

Grab a good friend to get into it. This can make the process much more fun. Jeremiah and Alex handed over the fate of their rooms to each other, for better or worse. Turns out, they knew each other pretty well.

Easy Does It

Trying to color inside the lines? It's tough when you're painting a wall trim or a cool design. Here are some tips to help you out:

1. Outline what you want to paint with painter's tape. Press down on the tape so it's totally stuck to the wall.

2. For control, choke up on the paintbrush, holding it at the base of the handle, close to the bristles.

3. Easy does it. Don't press too hard!

Quick Quiz

How well do you know your best friend?

1. If your friend had to live with ONE (yes, one!) color for the rest of their life, what would it be?

2. If your friend could add one thing to their room, what would it be?

3. If your friend could trash one big thing in their room, what would it be?

4. Your friend likes:
   a) antiques
   b) funky retro items
   c) anything new, new, new

Give each other the quiz and compare answers!

Off the Hook

Are your clothes starting to eat your closet? Looking to clear some space? It's simpler than you think. For starters, not everything needs to be kept on a hanger. You can fold pants and T-shirts and throw them in plastic storage bins or crates. It's a cheap and neat way to change the fate of an exploding closet. (You'll probably find you have extra room to fill up all over again!)

Craft, Create & Construct

Time to get crafty! Channel your inner carpenter and let's get to work. Here are some simple how-to's to make your new room totally you.

Mark My Words

Want to ask people to knock before entering? Have a favorite saying or band? Let the words do the talking with a little paint, a piece of wood or cardboard, and some stencils.

Here's what you do:

1. Decide what you want your sign to say.
2. Grab a piece of wood or cardboard and if you want a blast of background color, paint it.
3. Pick out stencils. They come in all sizes and designs at stationery or craft stores.
4. Make sure there's enough room to fit the letters by writing them lightly in pencil.
5. Place your stencils, hold them tight, and dab the paint carefully with a brush or sponge.
6. Gently lift the stencil and let it dry.
7. Hang the signs. (You might want to ask an adult to help you out!)

Let your words speak for themselves!

Hands Down, The Oscar Goes To . . .
Make an Impression

If you wanna feel like a star, do as the stars do. You can create your own Hollywood-like imprints with style and flair. (And you don't even need to use cement!)

Here's how:

1. Get some red or gray clay.
2. Mold the clay into thick, flat slabs no thinner than 2 inches. Make sure there's enough room for your hand!
3. Press your hand and all your fingers firmly into the slab and remove it carefully.
4. Add color and shine by pressing beads, stones, or sea glass into the clay, molding the clay around the objects to hold them in place.
5. Let your creation dry and place it in a special spot in your room. Create a roster of "stars" by having your friends, family, or pets add their imprints, too.

Super Shagadelic
Change the Fabric

In the 1970s, shag carpeting was all the rage. The superfuzzy stuff filled people's homes from wall to wall in colors like orange, avocado, and brown! Designer Scott used the shag carpet look to cover the ski lift chair in Jeremiah's room.

Want to add retro accents to your room? The simplest way is to find materials with funky colors and designs. You can use a staple gun or upholstery tacks to attach the fabric around the bottom of a chair. Or you can drape the material across your bed, hang it over a doorway, or use it to cover a toy chest.

After measuring the fabric, Scott and the girls hung the chair from the ceiling. It won't take Jeremiah up the slopes, but it's definitely a cool place to sit.

Funky See, Funky Do
Add Some Color

Want to make some bold choices for your own room, but painting the place gold, installing skateboard shelves, or bringing in a ski lift chair is NOT an option?

Try this:

1. Place a cool throw rug at the foot of your bed or on an angle in the middle of the room. You could even hang it on your wall.
2. Snag some throw pillows — try bold colors like magenta, red, indigo blue — and use them to liven up an old bedspread.
3. Paint the molding around your windows and door frames in a fun and funky color that stands out against your wall color. Or just paint the doors!

13

Kimmie

Kimmie, age 10, is seriously into sports.

For Jason's room redo, Kimmie kept it in the family. Her older sister Stephanie, who also knows her way around a soccer field, helped her redecorate Jason's room using some grrrrrl power!

Stephanie

Kimmie and Stephanie were totally into the *Trading Spaces* spirit, too. As they put it, "Look out, Jason. Here we come!"

Chapter 2

SOCCER FIELD

Do you have sports on the brain 24/7? Kimmie sure does. She needed a room that would put her right in the "in" zone — an all-out sports-themed space that goes way beyond dumping a few trophies on a shelf.

KICKIN' IT

"The first day after the show, I woke up and was like, 'This is my room?' But the second day, I knew." — Kimmie

14

1970S LOUNGE

Do you like to kick back and chill after school? Take a break from homework and listen to your favorite mixes? Jason wanted a pad he could lay back and groove out in — a throwback to the funkiest of 1970s style.

BOOGIE-DOWN LOUNGE

"I knew they were going to do my dream room, but I didn't know it was going to be this good!"
— Jason

Whose room is this?

Jason

Jason, age 9, gets his groove on to hip-hop and disco.

Jason chose to partner up with his friend Dillon.

Dillon

Together, they were ready to bust a few moves to get Kimmie's room done right.

KIMMIE'S CRIB RE-CREATED!

Without much prodding, Kimmie confesses: "My dream room would be sports, a lot of sports — 'cause I'm really good at it and I like it a lot." She's certainly got the trophies to prove it! We're thinking Kimmie was just a tiny tot when she started playing. But do the ruffles in her old room work well with her love of sports? Not quite.

Pretty & Purple, But Not QUITE Right

Keeping It Real

Why do people assume that if you're a girl you like pink, and if you're a guy you like blue? It starts before we're even born, when people buy different clothes depending on the gender of baby-to-be. What's up with that? It's nothing but old-school stereotypes.

We suggest this: No matter which colors you choose, just like everything else in your room, they should be *your* choice. There are all sorts of ways to see color. Pink doesn't have to be just plain ol' baby pink and blue doesn't have to be the usual hue.

BEFORE

This shade of purple is pretty — but it's more fairy princess than Olympic athlete.

One-size ruffle does *not* fit all.

"It had so many flowers and it was off-white and plain. It made me feel bored." — Kimmie

With designer Jordin acting as referee, Jason and Dillon kick up some dust and get ready to whip this room into shape.

Kimmie's room went from frills with no thrills to a gold-medal winner! That's because Jason and Dillon know Kimmie as a trophied champion. Together, Jordin and the boys grabbed hold of the torch and headed for the finish line with a virtual indoor soccer field.

Jordin's mind went wild with ideas for Kimmie's room. Judging from the tennis ball sun and the light blue paint on the walls, the sky was the limit.

She's Got GAME

AFTER

Back in the Day: AstroTurf

The grass is always greener in sports stadiums...because it's not real! That fake, spiky green stuff, AstroTurf, was actually the result of a 1950s study that proved country kids were in better shape than city kids. Why? City kids had fewer places to play and run around. The solution? "Invent" fake grass. At first, it was called Chemturf. But once the Houston Astros started their 1966 baseball season on it, they decided to rename it for themselves — AstroTurf!

JASON'S DIGS REDONE!

Is your room boredom central? Does it seem like all you do in there is homework and sleep? Scott and the girls placed Jason's music interests front and center by throwing down a dance floor and putting up a DJ booth. Now when Jason is done with the H-work, his room isn't only about catching some Zzz's.

Consider THIS

You can place your hobbies and interests on the front burner, too — and you don't need a dance floor to do it. Remember that easel you pull out every now and then? Why not set it up in your room for a 24-hour-a-day art studio? Or that guitar you got for your birthday? Lean it up against the wall where you can see it. Place your boom box nearby, and wah-la! A virtual recording studio where you can jam to your favorite tunes.

Got the message? Surround yourself with things you like to do. These are the things that will keep you revived and energized!

The stars are OK, but they're not exactly chill.

BEFORE

Umm, hey, where's he gonna dance? On his desk?

"I want a place where I can...hang out and dance and listen to music."
— Jason

Cleanup time! Jason's mom reports that Jason, who hadn't exactly been "into" housecleaning before, now has a special broom that he uses to clean his dance floor — ALL THE TIME.

18

Consider THAT

Music isn't important to everyone. But for those who can't live without it, music makes or breaks the atmosphere. Rock, hip-hop, country, pop, classical . . . whatever the flavor, it's music that sets the tone. And you may not realize it but music is also full of ideas.

All music has a history — running themes of style, color, and mood. Check it out. Do some research. Or just consider "the look" of the music, then make it your own. You can even mix your other interests with your taste in tunes. Dig the colors on that CD case? Use them to accent your bookshelf! Or trace that design on the concert T-shirt you got last summer and use it as a stencil.

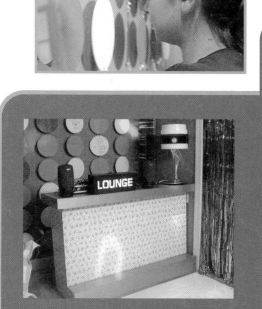

AFTER

Back in the Day: The DJ Booth

Hey, Mr. DJ . . . In the 1940s, the first DJs emerged as entertainers for soldiers overseas. It was World War II, and hiring one person was a lot cheaper than hiring an entire band! So people armed with a turntable, a stackful of records, and a basic amplifier would entertain troops in mess halls by playing the most popular hits.

Jason wanted a real chill pad, and he got it.

"Burn, baby, burn . . . Disco Inferno!"

Into the Groove

Jason's blue stars were stripped from the wall to make way for a seventies-style, hip-hop dance lounge. Now Jason's room is the place to be.

19

Peel, Paint & Ponder

If you've planned your room carefully, everything should move quickly and easily, just like Kimmie's and Jason's rooms. From breaking it down to putting it back together — planning is the key!

Checkin' In

Before getting started, designers Scott and Jordin consulted Kimmie and Jason about what kinds of things they were most into. The two friends both had to be supersure about what the other liked. Luckily, they had time to talk it out before the *Trading Spaces* crew took their rooms apart!

Sometimes it might *seem* like your friends have a better clue about what you like than you do, but chances are you know best. Whether it's hockey and science or Shakespeare and ballet, it's worth it to check in by checking yourself out.

Kimmie's room redo goes smoothly after some careful planning.

Scott and the girls even have time to limbo as they load in Jason's new stuff!

Safety Tip #1: Loading Out / Loading In

Need to move a hefty piece of furniture? Even if you feel sure you can do it alone, why break your back trying? Grab another pair of hands. If it's huge, grab two pairs. When lifting the weight, bend your knees and don't arch your back. Before you lift, make sure to plan your route. Seems obvious, right? But you'd be surprised how many know-it-alls move something by themselves, only to cry later, "Oh, my achin' back!"

Let There Be Light!

Want to transform the look and feel of your room with the flip of a switch? Lighting is the simplest way to reset the mood of any room.

You don't need a lot of money to plug in a cool new atmosphere for your room. Try white or blue holiday lights. Hang or tack them to a door or window frame. Create a border around your bookshelf with them. This will make the room feel "warm and chill," as Scott would say. For a more sophisticated or fun look, you can use paper lanterns or plastic string lights. They come in all shapes, colors, and styles. And remember: Where you place the light is important. Try it different ways.

Dillon basks in the soccer ball's glow.

Flashing colored lights add an energetic vibe.

Craft, Create & Construct

Tick-Tack-Go!

Create a hanging ticktacktoe board on your wall. All you'll need is some Velcro, glue, Ping-Pong balls, and white spray paint.

Here's how:

1. Buy a sheet of Velcro. Cut the soft side of it into a square measuring 20 inches on all four sides.
2. Take the sheet outside and, using the end of a newspaper as a guide, spray paint two lines down from top to bottom and two lines across. There's your ticktacktoe board. Let it dry.
3. Cut the rough-side Velcro into strips.
4. Glue a strip of the Velcro (rough side out) around each Ping-Pong ball. Crisscross two more strips so they're really covered.
5. Grab a friend, stand a few feet away, and plan your strategy.

Ready to play?

Against the Grain?

Never. Capable carpenter Ginene knows that when sanding a piece of wood, always work with the grain. Sanding against it leaves scratches that will show up later, especially if you stain the wood.

Score!

You can create your own scoreboard with a piece of wood, black spray paint, and white paint or tape. Oh, and of course, numbers. How else would you keep the score?

The Outside In

Do rainy days bum you out? Make you feel itchy to move some muscles and blast a few past the goalie? Just because your room is inside the house doesn't mean it has to feel all caged in. If you're happier doing things outside, then it's time to bring the outside in.

* See what's covering your windows. Are they blocked by a bunch of junk — or do dark drapes keep the light out? Try a lighter curtain, or use ties to keep them open. Anything to shed a little light!

* Get a clear or colored jar. Next time you're on a camping trip, at the beach, or just hanging out in the neighborhood, pick up a rock, leaf, shell, abandoned golf ball — whatever grabs your attention. Place the stuff in a jar and put it in a spot that you're sure to see every day.

* Grab a map from your family's last road trip. Hang it on your wall, and mark the places you stopped. There you have it — an instant reminder of your time spent roughing it on the road.

Too Many Trophies?

You can never have too many! But should you throw those trophies up high on a shelf so that no one can mess with them? And so that you can never see them...? Not a chance!

You earned those beauties, right? So ditch the old dust-gathering routine and give your prizes and plaques the star treatment they deserve. And don't just think wood for shelving. You can use glass or plastic if you want your trophies to shimmer and shine. Try spreading them out like Kimmie has. If it's medals you've got, why not screw hooks into the wall and hang them? Thumbtacks might work, too.

JAZZY Jordin — Diva Designer!

"Don't be afraid to express yourself. And don't try to follow everyone else, because trends come and go, but style is timeless."

FULL NAME: Jordin Ruderman

WHAT SHE DOES ON *Trading Spaces: Boys vs. Girls*
Jordin is one-half the team of *Trading Spaces'* can-do designers. She's the "if you can dream it, she can dream it bigger" girl. Jordin has too much imagination to let herself be boxed in. She's designed everything from an awesome Arabian princess palace to a soccer-themed pad with AstroTurf walls to a New York City skyline room.

BACK IN THE DAY
Jordin follows in the footsteps of her grandmother, mother, and aunt, who were all interior decorators and antique dealers.

TRAINING
But Jordin never wanted to be a designer! She went to college for art history, and went on to get her Masters of Fine Arts in theater at Columbia University. While pursuing her acting career, she also started designing sets and costumes for the theater. Even though she had avoided design before that, she discovered that she enjoyed it!

IDEAS YOU CAN USE
"Think of all of your favorite things — what are you passionate about? Think about your favorite color, food, places you've been, places you'd like to go, or your favorite after-school activity. Then, out of the two, or three, or million interests you have, which ones pop out as ideas that you could really live with? Use these ideas as a starting point for a look or theme. You may not think you know anything about design, but of course you do — you have an opinion. That's all the knowledge you need."

ADVICE
"It's okay to be different. I never dressed like any other kid. I wore things like purple fringed sweat suits with hot-pink hiking boots made out of suede. I got teased a lot — especially in my teenage years. I didn't care. I just let it roll off my back. I liked being different. And it really helped shape who I am now."

SNAZZY Scott, Designing Dude!

"Every week we think Scott's lost his mind. Then we see the room, and we're like, 'Whoa!'"
—Diane

FULL NAME: Scott Sicari

WHAT HE DOES ON *Trading Spaces: Boys vs. Girls*

If it's out there, over the top, pushing the design envelope, chances are Scott did it! Scott is *Trading Spaces'* own Mr. Outrageous. He's hung ski lift chairs from the ceiling and transformed a plain pad into a rain forest haven.

BACK IN THE DAY

Way back when, the walls of Scott's very first room were covered with painted toy soldiers, and he stored his playthings in a soldier-shaped toy chest. Scott's dad fostered his love for creating different environments. He and his dad often constructed things together, like Halloween haunted houses — a spooky tradition that lasted for years and helped Scott learn the tricks of the trade.

TRAINING

After his dad taught him to think outside the box, Scott attended the University of the Arts in Philadelphia and majored in graphic design. From there, he turned to designing sets for TV and music videos, and lots of his wild ideas on *Trading Spaces: Boys vs. Girls* are inspired by different videos he worked on, from Whitney Houston to 'N Sync. It's not hard to see that this daring designer has a rock-and-roll edge — an edge that has helped him create some of the coolest rooms going!

IDEAS YOU CAN USE

Scott's always got designing on the brain, even when he's pursuing other hobbies. In one trip to a ski mountain, he scored an old ski lift chair and some snowboards. He kept his eyes open, talked to people, and made their old junk new again.

ADVICE

Scott isn't afraid to try new things in the rooms he designs. Orange paint, faux fur, pineapple lamps — have no fear! If he likes the Hawaiian print on his shorts, he makes a stencil of them and paints it on the wall. Inspiration can come from the most unexpected places. Try it!

Danielle

Danielle, age 11, goes wild for nature and animals.

Abby

Danielle teamed up with her friend Abby to create some supercool concepts for Garrett's new digs.

Chapter 3

RAIN FOREST

Imagine opening your bedroom door and stepping into a tropical rain forest. Danielle wanted a dream room where she could feel nurtured by nature. Her passion for pets put her in sync with the wilder side of life — a jungle's worth of creatures great and small.

LIONS AND TIGERS AND BEARS — OH MY!

"I think Danielle's dream would be having a forest, with waterfall noises." — Garrett

BASKETBALL COURT

Does the foul line seem too far from home? Garrett had trouble leaving the hoop in his driveway when he had four empty walls in his bedroom. He wanted round-the-clock layups and free throws! Luckily, his friends Danielle and Abby were on it. They transformed his room into an NBA-worthy arena!

HOOP DREAMS

"Garrett's dream room would include having a half basketball court." — Danielle

DANIELLE'S CRIB RE-CREATED!

Danielle digs flowers, but her interest in the wild wonders of nature have no place to grow in this prim and proper pad.

Kind of cute, but these cuddly creatures aren't exactly livin' large in that basket!

Time to Organize

Frighteningly FLORAL

Searching for something to do with your often-overlooked stuffed animals?
When things sit in the same spot for a long time, you can almost forget they're there. The trick is to showcase your pals in an interesting new way.

Scott surveyed Danielle's varied collection of cuddly creatures and decided they fit right in with a woodsy landscape. Although we haven't done a head count, it looks like not a single stuffed animal was sent packing.

Hmmm, Danielle, would these be the flowers you're a little sick of?

BEFORE

"(My room) hasn't been done since I was little and I really am sick of the flowers that are there." — Danielle

Quaint and cute, but ready for a bigger home.

Here are some ideas for your own zoo:

• Give 'em room to breathe. Don't stuff your animals into one tight spot — spread them out!

• Find out more about your animals — what species they are, what environment they're used to. Then use that info in your room.

• If you have a stuffed snake like Danielle does, wrap it around your bedpost. A bird could be perched on a bookshelf. Got lions, tigers, and bears? Create some forest scenery to place behind them. All you need is some construction paper, markers, and crayons to create a cool picture.

Treetops and Furry FRIENDS

Danielle has a full house in her forest fortress, complete with a collection of creatures to keep her company while she's hangin' in the jungle.

AFTER

Danielle's reaction a few weeks later? "I find new things every day."

The Real Deal: Rain Forests

- **Home, sweet home:** Rain forests cover only six percent of Earth's landmasses — but house more than half of the plant and animal species on the planet.

- **The forest for the trees:** Tropical rain forests have so many trees in them that rain doesn't actually hit the ground — it rolls down branches and trunks in a misty spray.

- **No snow days?** Tropical rain forests have no "seasons" — no dry spells or cold periods when things don't grow. It's hot and rainy all the time!

Diane is amazed with the Amazon-like results!

How did they think of that?

Inspiration for the tree trunk bed actually came from a music video! Years ago, Scott was the set designer for a Whitney Houston video that had a three-tiered stage in the middle of the woods. Now, lucky Danielle has a forest nook of her very own!

GARRETT'S DIGS REDONE!

Garrett's current room is way out of bounds. Definitely lacking the alley-oop to make a slam dunk of his digs.

Danielle, Abby, and Jordin have some serious work to do here. Between pulling up the carpet, repainting the walls, and installing a Murphy bed, can they manage to transform this place in 48 hours? There's no overtime in *Trading Spaces*!

Consider THIS

You know how in the last days of summer you prep yourself for the new school year by updating your wardrobe? You're a year older, and you want your clothing to show it. Makes sense.

Then why do most of us let our rooms stay in the not-so-recent past? Probably because it seems like changing a room is such a big task, and we wonder if it's worth the time.

Time-out! Something as simple as moving the furniture, framing a long-lost picture, or putting a new comforter on the bed can take mere moments out of your day. And they will change your crib for the rest of the year.

BEFORE

Nice attempt, but with a little more team spirit this room could really soar.

Not what you'd expect from a major NBA fan!

"I want my room redecorated, because it was done when I was, like, four, and I think it needs to be older, more like my age." — Garrett

In the Know

Danielle and Abby really enjoyed their late-night painting homework on day one. And their least favorite moments of Garrett's room redo? "Pulling up a carpet and pulling staples out of the floor — that wasn't very fun," Danielle says.

Garrett made a fast break to his new bedroom. Now when he takes a time-out from homework he can slam a few hook shots to unwind.

Consider THAT

These bleacher-style benches give new meaning to the phrase "box seats." Danielle and Abby both put storage at the top of the priority list.

Looks like Garrett is up against some stiff competition!

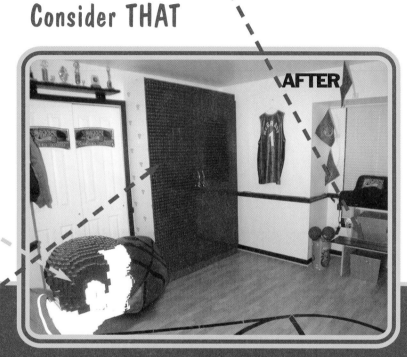

AFTER

Back in the Day: The Murphy Bed

Necessity is the mother of invention, they say. But what are they really talking about? William L. Murphy knows. It's all about inventing something because you N-E-E-D it. That's Murphy's story. He wanted to have friends over to visit, but he had no room for them to sleep. So he started toying with the idea of a folding bed. Wah-la! In 1900, the Murphy bed was born. And it caught on, too. Turns out, a lot of people had too many friends and not enough space, and Murphy's invention was the perfect solution.

Peel, Paint & Ponder

Jordin and the girls are big fans of Garrett's. And they decided that he should be surrounded by fans all the time. Which brings us to...

The Mural of the Story

Paint isn't your only option. There are lots of reasons people decide to go with wallpaper and murals. They can be hard work to put up, but the advantages are worth it.

- There are countless patterns to pick from. Wallpaper allows us to use patterns and designs that we couldn't paint on our own.

- Photographic murals can transport you beyond the four walls of your bedroom.

- Wallpaper can sometimes give your room a texture that paint can't offer.

Makin' Ends Meet

When gluing two things together, most people think the more you use, the more it glues. Not so! Thin layers are best. The point of glue is to help two surfaces stick together. If you glob on the glue, the two sides are less likely to meet in the middle.

After applying a thin layer of glue, lightly glide a piece of cardboard or the edge of a thick piece of paper along the surface to smooth the glue out and take off any extra goo. You can also use your index finger if you don't mind having sticky fingers.

Wallpaper up...and the crowd goes wild!

Measure for Measure

You can never measure too much. Breaking out the ruler or tape measure can take you that extra mile. Better measurements help you do a better job. They give your creative work a more professional look. And if you're building something, it'll probably last longer, too!

Making the Cut

Have you ever grabbed something that needed to be cut to size and started snipping away with the scissors, only to find that your straight line zigged and zagged?

Even if you have a good eye and a steady hand, your cut can be on the down slope. So, anytime you need to snip something, outline it first. Use a ruler for straight lines and a stencil or pattern for the intricate stuff. Practice can help, too! Try cutting your shape on a piece of scrap paper before you slice and dice the valued object.

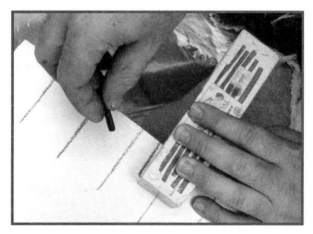

Don't have a ruler handy? Any straight edge (like this box) will work.

Safety Tip #2: Googly Goggles

Contrary to popular belief, goggles are *not* dorky. They're a symbol of how tough you are! And they're useful, too. They keep the dust from settling where it shouldn't, and they ensure that both eyeballs stay in your head. So, next time you need to spray paint or sand, slide 'em on.

Craft, Create & Construct

There are lots of easy ways to personalize your room. So what are you waiting for?

Above the Rim

Feel like your mini hoop has lost all hope? Does it need a little edge? Why not set your sights above the rim and personalize your backboard? You can give it a winning look by using decals and stickers of your favorite team logos. You can also paint funky designs, using a non-water-based paint (it'll last longer). Or try a little graffiti art with different colored spray paints.

Danielle and Abby decided to decal the doors!

Into the Wild
Know Your Plants

Want to get a feel for the forest? You can incorporate elements of a lush landscape by exercising your green thumb and placing plants around your room.

Take a trip to the local nursery and check out these easy-to-care-for plants:

Ivy — Grows quickly and spreads out all over the place. You can wrap or drape the vines around a bedpost or bookshelf.

Boston Ferns — Fantastically green and woodsy.

Norfolk Island Pines — Can get pretty tall — buy a bunch, let them grow, and use them as room dividers.

Oxalis — This tropical/subtropical plant has leaves that open during the day and close at night.

Just Stuff It

Sew a Pillow

Got an old jersey that no longer fits? Just can't toss that winning tee? Sew it up and stuff it! Jordin and the girls found a jersey from Garrett's home team and used it to create comfort with a terrific twist — they turned it into a pillow!

The Sixers have gone soft — into a pillow, that is!

1. Decide what size you want your pillow to be.
2. Cut the length of the shirt to size, leaving about an inch of extra material. Do the same with the sleeves.
3. Sew up the bottom of the shirt and the sleeve openings but be sure to leave an opening — the neckline, for example — for the stuffing.
4. Stuff your shirt with filler (from a craft store) and sew up the opening.

Hittin' the Court & Playin' the Field

Floor It!

It only takes a little bit of planning and concentration to put yourself in the center of the playing field. Paint is pretty permanent, so try using tape instead — it's temporary, just in case you change your mind.

Try this:

1. Use black or green colored tape.
2. On a piece of paper, draw the court or field lines you want on your floor and decide where they will go.
3. Use a white China Marker or grease pencil to draw the lines on the floor. There's no need to press hard. Use a light touch, just enough so that you can step back and see a trace of the line.
4. Does it look right? Are your lines straight? Are your curves correct? If so, place the tape down directly on top of your tracing lines. Make sure all of the tape is fully pressed down.

Question: What can you do with a wood floor, other than throw down a rug?

Answer: You can create a cool basketball or tennis court, baseball diamond or hockey field.

When you're finished, have a field day! You'll always have the home court advantage!

Taylor

Taylor, age 9, is an aspiring actress with a soft side for anything hippie.

Nicole

Taylor and her best friend, Nicole, made waves with their design ideas for Mark's beach blanket bungalow. They kicked up some sand and got ready to bask on the beach!

Chapter 4

HIPPIE HAVEN

Does the style and spirit of the sixties' peace movement inspire you? Taylor's rainbow revelations of peace, love, and unity needed the perfect pitch. She longed to have a hippie haven of her own.

FAR-OUT

"Taylor's a girl who likes to have a lot of fun."
— Mark

HAWAIIAN HIDEAWAY

Are you better on the beach? Mark is! His love of surfing and sandy shores makes him the perfect candidate for a handsome Hawaiian hideaway — a relaxed refuge where he can sit back and strum his guitar.

SURF'S UP!

"Mark really likes to play on the beach and surf. He really likes the water." — Nicole

Whose room is this?

Mark

Mark, age 13, has some fancy footwork on the court, but his passion is playing guitar.

Matt

Mark invited Matt along for Taylor's room redo — a real flower-power experience. They came up with some radical remedies to send Taylor back to the sixties!

TAYLOR'S CRIB RE-CREATED!

Taylor has theatrical tastes and a hankering for anything hippie. Mark says that Taylor digs lots of colorful things. So, where are they in her room? Looks like Taylor's space could use a colossal color explosion! Mark and Matt had better listen up: Not just any color will do. Taylor says, "The worst thing they could do to my room is turn everything pink, really hot pink."

Consider THIS

In the Mood

OK, so the plastic mood ring you got for your birthday reveals all you need to know about what colors match what moods, right? Not exactly. While some research shows that certain colors bring out specific moods, it seems that colors can mean different things to different people. One person's soothin' is another's sour mood.

How do you figure out your hue? Go back to that crayon box. Find the colors you like and use them to fill in a few plain white index cards — one color per card. Tape each card to a different wall of your room. Over the next few days, remind yourself to glance over at the patch of color. How does it make you feel? Inspired? Happy? Sad? Crabby? Calm? It's a great way to learn your response to a color without ever picking up a brush.

BEFORE

The writing's on the wall — this girl likes a burst of color!

Cute and sweet, but not very groovy.

"There was a light, light, light green bed with a pink bedspread, and that's my least favorite color." — Taylor

Taylor wanted to keep the bedspread, just not the pink. Now it's underneath a tie-dyed sheet.

In the Know

How did Jordin feel about designing this peace pad?
"I love this room! Especially the curtains. I've done two rooms with beaded curtains, and I love them so much — I must get some for my own house!"

Perfect PEACE Pad

Taylor has seen the dawning of the age of Aquarius — right in her own bedroom! The lime-green accents are gone and a new peace mobile has been added to take her for a radical ride back in time.

AFTER

Groovy messages "Blowin' in the Wind."

The incredible, nonedible egg.

Back in the Day: The Smiley Face

Jordin and the guys put on a happy face in Taylor's room — but where did it come from? In 1963, an insurance company in Massachusetts needed a way to cheer up gloomy employees. They asked artist Harvey Ball to come up with artwork that would remind people to smile. At first he drew just the smile — but then realized that it "frowned" if he turned it upside down. So he added a pair of eyes, and the smiley face was born.

Taylor: "My radiator was terrible because I painted it purple one time and it kind of got all marked up, but now it's a hippie bus." All aboard!

Jordin and company are not about to put up pink of any kind — phew!

39

MARK'S DIGS REDONE!

Wood paneling and dark green carpet? That's about as far from the beach as you can get. Seems kinda closed off and closed in, especially for a guy who likes ocean breezes in the air and sand beneath his feet.

Mark isn't the only one unsatisfied with his stomping ground. Taylor calls it "dark and dull and messed up." (Tell us what you really think, Taylor!)

He Said . . .

Mark: "The worst thing the girls could do to my room is..."
Matt: "...make it purple or pink..."
Mark: "...or make it..."
Matt: "...Barbie-ish."

She Said . . .

Taylor: "Mark kept telling me, 'I'm gonna redo your room in Barbie and G.I. Joe!'"

LOW tide

BEFORE

Kind of conservative for a laid-back guy.

Strolling on this carpet is no day at the beach.

"My ultimate dream room would be a Hawaiian theme, where I could just kick back and relax, and also where I could get away from the world." — Mark

In the Know: Dress to Impress

Regular viewers of *Trading Spaces: Boys vs. Girls* have surely noticed Jordin's and Scott's ever-changing styles — their clothes usually match the themes of the rooms they're decorating. One week, Jordin's in a lifeguarding outfit, the next she's a referee. And Scott will don anything from surf shorts to plastic rock-and-roller pants to get in the spirit.

Jordin actually has a history of dressing in themes. To support herself through college, Jordin got a job delivering pizza. To make the job more interesting, she and a friend decided to dress up differently every day. They'd go as Thelma and Louise, or witches, or fortune-tellers. Jordin laughs, "We spent all the money we made delivering pizza buying the costumes for the next week!"

TOTALLY Tropical

Are you a beach bum who digs the sand and surf? A daring dude who watches for wild waves? A lady who lounges in swimsuits and flip-flops? Do you wait all year for summer vacation so you can set your sights on the sea?

Try painting ocean waves on your wall. Take those seashells you've been collecting and lay them out on a shelf, or try gluing a few to a picture frame. Paint the colors of a sunset over your headboard. You don't have to wait for summer break to catch an ocean breeze!

AFTER

Fun, festive lighting sets the tone.

Is this Mark's bedroom or a vacation location?

Surf's up!

The Real Deal: The Pineapple

Aside from the fact that it looks cool, why would Scott put a pineapple lamp in Mark's room? For one, it totally plays into the tropical theme. This fruit was a favorite of the Carib Indians, who brought the treat from Paraguay and Brazil, where it was known as *anana*, or "excellent fruit." Explorers introduced it to European culture, and Charles II of England even posed for an official portrait in which he was receiving a pineapple as a gift. The prickly fruit became a symbol of hospitality in the American colonies — people even "rented" confectionery pineapples for a day if they really wanted to impress.

Before, Mark wanted to bail on his bedroom. But he's all over his new Hawaiian hideout. He can even hang back with homework at his tiki hut desk.

Peel, Paint & Ponder

Jordin suggested a rainbow theme, since the colorful arch was a symbol of hippie harmony. Do you dig it?

Time and Time Again

Have you singled out the 1960s like Taylor has? Does the Renaissance rev you up? Are you excited about the eighties? Thrilled by the thirties? A lot of people connect with a specific era. Wanna bring the past into your present? A little research can take you back and move you forward. Looking at pictures in a bookstore, library, or online can get you that much closer to the era you love most. Some fab ideas for your own retro room redo might be just a photograph away!

Color My Decade

Color is not totally timeless. Like clothing styles and furniture fads, some colors are more popular during certain times than others.

For example:

1920s: flappers flipped over anything silver and gold.

1970s: focused on combinations of brown, beige, and orange.

1980s: made a palette of pastels popular and gave new meaning to the color black.

Depending on your decade of choice, you can use these colors as bases or accents — and no matter how you arrange them, they'll all flow together in your own personal way. Now that's cool.

Let's Hear from You

What's your favorite era?

"I have a seventies poster and a few dress-up costumes and posters....It makes me feel I belong in a group...a seventies group." — Abby, 9

"I'm liking this one. I don't really have a time period. Now, I like the style better. It's cool." — Michael, 12

Lost & Found: Attics and Basements

OK, so you know your era and you've got some ideas. Now it's time to incorporate the past with the present. Know the saying "one person's trash is another person's treasure"? Take a look in your own basement or attic — treasures can be hidden up above or down below. Chances are pretty good that there's a hidden gem that you could give a terrific new twist to.

Mark got really tired of looking at this ol' dresser, but someone else might savor it.

Scott uses his surf shorts as inspiration for Mark's wall.

Dress It Up

If you're like most people, you probably wear your tastes on your sleeve. Take a look at your clothing choices — you can use the patterns and colors of your favorite threads to decorate your walls! Scott even donated his shorts for the *Trading Spaces* occasion!

1. On a flat surface, press a sheet of tracing paper against your clothing pattern. Lightly trace the pattern lines with a pen or marker. Be careful not to tear the paper!

2. Turn the tracing paper over and retrace the lines on the back with a soft lead or charcoal pencil. No need to be neat. Just make sure the lines are fully covered on the back side.

3. Place the back of the tracing paper against the wall where you want your pattern to be and retrace the lines with a rounded pen cap. Press hard enough to leave your mark on the wall, but not so hard that you tear through the paper.

4. When you pull the paper away, your design should be on the wall! Now paint over the lines to give it a polished look.

Jordin is a master at breathing new life into the old. For Taylor's peace pad, she bought the light at a second-hand store, and found the egg chair on the street.

Lost & Found: Yanking from Yard Sales

Is your basement bare? Was your attic cleared out and swept clean? If your treasure hunt turned up nothing but a little dust, check out some yard sales. Your neighbors might have just the things you're looking for. You can snag the funkiest finds for a fraction of your allowance! Or take a trip to a cheapie antiques store, and remember not to overlook the small stuff. An old, empty string bean can from your favorite time period can cost fifty cents — and you can use it as a pencil cup! It's all in the details!

Craft, Create & Construct

Something Shady

Mark and Matt wanted to dress up Taylor's room with messages of unity, peace, and love. Jordin asked the guys to create a design around those three words of wisdom where everyone could see them — on Taylor's window shades. You, too, can sassy up some sagging shades with your own messages or designs.

Here's how:

* Use acrylic paint on fabric shades. You can paint your words or pictures directly onto the shade, or design a pattern on a piece of paper first. For words, paint freestyle with hand and brush. For lettering, paint with a brush or cut letters out of thin kitchen sponges, dip them into the paint, and press them onto your shade.

* Use permanent markers on plastic shades. You can draw and write your way to a snappier look for your shades. It's easy, and there are endless marker colors to pick from!

To "Dye" For

Tie-dye your way to a groovy new look. Jordin gave the guys full reign over the dyeing of Taylor's pillowcases, but you can tie-dye just about any material you want!

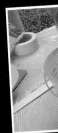

Here's how:

1. Soak the material in cool water and ring it out.

2. Twist the material into a ball with your hands, and use rubber bands to keep it tightly wound.

3. Place it in a sodium carbonate (washing soda) solution for 20 minutes.

4. While you wait, pick your favorite colors and prepare the dyes, following the instructions on the package.

5. Dip your material in the dye, or squirt dye

Scott and the girls went wild down in Waikiki! They created a shady spot where Mark can do his schoolwork. Homework never felt so relaxing!

Totally Tiki

If you dig sand dunes and salty air and need a mellow place to work, consider taking your desk to the heights of tiki-dom.

Try these ideas:

1. You can buy three stalks of bamboo and cut them to create three-sided edging for your desk. Place one piece of bamboo along the back edge of the top of your desk and two along the sides. If you have a wooden desk, gently hammer in three or four small nails for each strip of bamboo. If your desk is made from another type of material, use epoxy glue to attach your bamboo. Get help with the epoxy, because it can be tricky and sticky.

2. Slip your desk into a hula skirt. Attach skirts of straw to the sides of your desk with a staple or glue gun.

3. Raffia is a straw material that's sold in bundles and comes in all sorts of cool colors. Spread glue on the face of a plain picture frame, pencil holder, or other desk accessory. Lay down strips of raffia side by side, on the glue. Trim off the edges and let it dry.

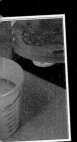

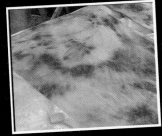

on it with a spray bottle. Then wrap it up in plastic and let it sit for at least 24 hours.

6. Rinse with cool water and detergent, then unwrap it — check out the pattern!

7. Rinse the unwrapped material in cool water and detergent again, until the water runs clear.

   HINT: Do not wash your creation with other items.

8. Lay your new creation out to dry!

Safety Tip #3: The Glove Department

Don't disrespect your digits — protect them with gloves! Whenever you're working with chemicals — varnish, turpentine, or any other agent — make sure you wear the appropriate gloves for the task at hand. Some chemicals require thicker gloves, so always check out the safety label for instructions. Protect all ten fingers so you'll be on hand to give your room the snappy attention it deserves.

Nicki

Nicki, age 13, is a dreamer with a love for travel and anything exotic.

Mia

Nicki teamed up with her friend Mia to get Nat's room afloat.

Chapter 5

ARABIAN PALACE

Travel by land or by sea while staying within the four walls of your bedroom!

You don't need a passport to work your way around the globe. Just use a little creativity, roll up your sleeves, and put some muscle into it. Nat and Nicki did. Nat, along with friend Daniel and designer Jordin, brought Nicki's room to a whole new world.

MAGIC CARPET RIDE

"Since Nicki likes to travel, we thought that she might like a Moroccan kind of room."
— Daniel

CAPTAIN'S QUARTERS

In turn, Nicki brought Scott and her friend Mia onboard to give Nat a view of the high seas from the hull of a pirate's ship.

Before the redos, Nat and Nicki weren't sure how their rooms would turn out. They admitted to being a little nervous. But everything worked out perfectly. "I am really happy about it," Nat says. "It feels a lot more like my room now." Nicki agrees. "It's really fun to be in...I like *everything*!"

AHOY, MATE!

"My nightmare room would be little kittens on the wall and big poufy pillows. I would like something that would fit my personality more." — Nat

Nat

Nat, age 11, is an adventurer with a passion for the high seas.

Daniel

Nat teamed up with buddy Daniel to take Nicki's room on a magic carpet ride.

NICKI'S CRIB RE-CREATED!

Nicki's parents deserve some props.
This room definitely took effort to put together, with its elaborate patterns of flower petals. Still, it hasn't been revamped in seven years and needs some serious updating. Nat thought the flowers were a little "babyish" and they don't really take Nicki where her grown-up tastes want to go.

The Inside Track: Boys vs. Girls

It's hard to hand over total control of your bedroom. Especially to two friends of the opposite gender. So how do the *Trading Spaces* kids handle it? Some were in total panic mode, while others were totally chill. Have a listen to what they said when we asked:

Were you nervous about having your friends redo your room?

Nicki: "Sort of, but I knew Jordin had done a really cool other room, so I knew my room would look cool, too."

Danielle: "I kind of got worried at first...."

Alex: "I trusted the boys. I knew they wouldn't go wild in my room because if they did then I would do that in their room."

Home Sweet HUMDRUM

BEFORE

Nat: "Nicki's room is really young. And the flowers need to go."

This pattern is perky, but not very promising for a traveling type.

Blooming, but a little boring.

"My nightmare room would be more flowers than I have right now. Yellows. Puke greens. I want something that's like a mixture of mature and exotic."
— Nicki

Eli: "I wasn't really nervous."

Megan: "I felt more comfortable because if someone I didn't even know had done it then they would put up something that I totally didn't like."

The geography here has got to change. Nicki's stuff needs a little direction.

Going GLOBAL!

Nicki's former flower motif received a shower of sophistication. In place of the gushing garden is an exotic palace with a diverse blend of cultural influences.

Nicki can take flight around the globe on her magic carpet bed or hang back and enjoy her dynasty of one.

Music never looked so good.

A magic carpet to take Nicki to wide-open spaces and faraway places!

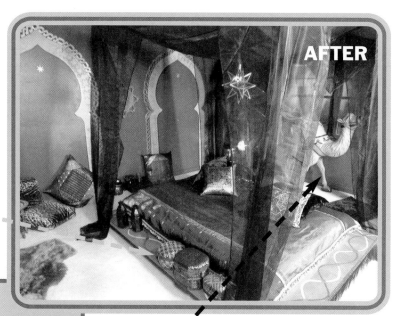

AFTER

The Real Deal: The Carousel

Flash way back to the 1100s, when Arab and Turkish horsemen liked to play a game on horseback. They were having fun, but when the Spanish saw it they called it "little war," or *carosella*. The French made the game more extravagant, and called it *carrousel*. They even had a contest to see who could race, on horseback, and grab a brass ring that hung from a tree branch. Then, about 300 years ago, a man from France decided to carve and hang wooden horses from chains around a center pole. They were moved in a circular motion by mule or manpower. Soon, all sorts of people wanted to ride the faux horses, just for fun. And merrily we've gone round and round ever since.

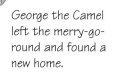

George the Camel left the merry-go-round and found a new home.

In the Know

What was the hardest part of redoing Nicki's room?
Nat: "At first, I was really nervous about everything. I said, 'I am not a skilled artist. How are we going to paint all that?'"

NAT'S DIGS REDONE!

Nat's mind sails at the mere thought of taking to the high seas. Unfortunately, though, his room is docked and anchored with its dull decor. Before *Trading Spaces* came along, "It was kind of bland and boring. It wasn't anything that anyone would want to look at," he says.

Scott dons pirate garb to put himself in the proper mood. After two days of hard work and low-down labor, Scott joked that he'd make Nat "walk the plank" if he doesn't like his room. No mutinies here!

Anchored and MAROONED

BEFORE

All hands on deck! We need to begin a radical makeover of this room.

Nautical, but not so noticeable!

"I think Nat needs his room redone. His walls are sort of plain."
— Nicki

This plaid bedspread was soon to be thrown overboard.

There were some details in Nat's room that were sea-worthy. Like the boat mobile, for one. Nat's mom also pointed out the wallpaper. OK, so Nat was off to a nautical start, but it was definitely time to set sail for more exciting places. . . .

A typical, unexciting work area doesn't float Nat's boat.

Pirate's PARADISE

Nat's dull den is replaced by a maritime miracle that would put even Captain Hook to shame. Every detail, from portholes to a mast in the middle of his room, was included in his new seafaring vessel. He can survey the sea from the deck, or hang out down below in the hull. The girls definitely got Nat back on course!

"Sea" your reflection through the porthole mirror.

Nat and his mates have a place to store their treasures.

AFTER

Back in the Day: The Figurehead

Sailing on the high seas was risky business. (Ever heard the phrase "man overboard"?) No wonder sailors sought good luck by attaching a figure at the head of their ships. For the boat's good-luck charm, they'd use everything from lions and unicorns to geese and bulls. Female figures began showing up after 1800, when the ships' owners would sometimes use their wives as models.

CAPTAIN'S QUARTERS

Captain Nat is ready for awesome adventures.

"I really, really like the desk and the poop deck. Behind the door they have pictures of different knots that the sailors used to tie — that's really cool." — Nat

In the Know

What was the hardest part of redoing Nat's room?
Nicki: "We put wood all over his walls and then we had to stain it, and it was really sticky. Once we did one coat, they decided it was too light, so we had to go around and do it all over again."

Peel, Paint & Ponder

Next Stop, Adventure!

Where do you want to go? Someplace real? Someplace imagined? Or somewhere that combines the two? Inspiration is everywhere: books, movies, myths. . . . Open up your mind to the possibilities. Whatever captures your imagination can be visited — and, with a little time and energy, re-created. Design, create, and color the world you've been dreaming about.

Around the World

Nicki's interest in other lands comes from her love of travel. Jordin and the guys conjured up a combination of the real (Moorish archways) and the fantastic (magic carpets). These were designed to transport Nicki to the far stretches of the globe and spark her infinite imagination. *Why not take your own journey?*

Try this:

• Explore the color schemes and materials that are constants in the cultures you're most captivated by — the rich silks and indigo blues of Arabia, the intricate calligraphy and artwork of the Far East, the snowy mountains of Switzerland. . . .

• Explore the shapes and design patterns that are common in the places you consider to be the coolest. Jordin and the guys used an arabesque arch pattern for Nicki's walls, creating the look of a palace fit for a queen.

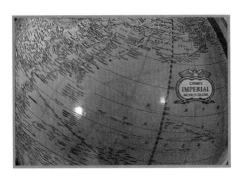

• Are you lucky enough to have visited a special place you adore? Hopefully, you or your family took some pictures. Try blowing up the photographs and hanging them on your walls. Presto! Your room is a whole new world!

Off the Shelf

Nat's interest in the nautical comes from reading the Horatio Hornblower books, fictitious stories set during the French Revolution. Do you have a book that engages you, keeps you reading from morning till night on a summer Saturday? Books that inspire don't have to be shelved when you're done reading them. You can re-create the book's world in your room and inhabit it 24/7.

1. Close your eyes and think about your favorite books. What do you picture?
2. Write down or draw all the images that come to mind.
3. Check out the list or drawings you've made. If you can picture it, you can probably paint it, craft it, and re-create it.

Fab Fabrics

Fabrics and materials come in all shapes and sizes. They have tons of uses, so why limit yourself? Jordin made Nicki's canopy out of Indian saris, a type of women's clothing that's usually made from silk. Try using fabric in different ways. You can buy all sorts of cool materials in pieces and "swatches" at a huge discount, too. Pay a visit to the fabric store and rummage through the sample and leftover bins. You may walk away with a buried treasure.

Cool as a Canopy

You don't need to have a four-poster bed to drape your sweet dreams in a canopy of colors. You can re-create the look with four sturdy hooks, some cool material, and a ladder (or very, very long arms!).

Jordin put the boys to work sewing the saris together for Nicki's canopy bed.

Safety Tip #4: Safety in Numbers

You may never in your life use a sewing machine or a power drill. But if you do, grab an adult who can help you learn the ropes. We're not suggesting a full-time chaperon — just someone who knows what they're doing. Learn to use tools correctly now and you'll be a master in no time. Then you'll be the one who's supervising. . . .

Craft, Create & Construct

Use It, Don't Lose It. Creating a cool environment doesn't have to mean buying new stuff. You can alter your perspective on the things you have by adding other materials to the mix. Here's how to turn those trips to the seashore into a table and shelves, and how to make over your bulletin board by tacking on a little personal expression!

Mad for Mosaics

Everything from tabletops to picture frames can be made more interesting and beautiful by adding your own eye-catching artwork. Making a mosaic is easier than it looks. If an item has a border or lip on all four sides, you can inlay stones, pieces of glass, coins, or tiles. Jordin, Nat, and Daniel used colorful polished glass beads to inlay tabletops.

Jordin and Nat pour their polished glass beads into the frame that lines the tabletop.

Next, they pour a clear cement resin (a gummy glue that will dry as a hard plastic) over the glass beads. They use a clean disposable paintbrush with bristles to smooth out the resin and make it even across the surface. This stuff works fast. It starts to harden in only 20 minutes, so they have to move quickly. Then it takes 24 hours to completely dry.

Consider This: Swept Ashore

Ever seen a piece of driftwood drying in the sand at the beach? These lucky pieces of wood emerge from the salty ocean water, sit in the sun, and bleach into the coolest hues of gray and white. And if the wood is dry and clean enough, you can use it as a shelf. What if you're land-locked and nowhere near the shoreline? You're in luck! There is a stain called "pickling white" that can be painted on a new piece of wood to give it that ocean-weathered look. Put your drift-wood up with anchors, a few screws, and a couple of brackets and you've got yourself a book-shelf with coastal character.

Consider That:
Expanding the Board-ers

Nicki wanted a new bulletin board — more space to pin and tack, and something that was out of the ordinary. Jordin and the guys came up with an elaborate design that shattered all assumptions about what a bulletin board should look like. But you can transform a simple square or rectangular corkboard, too.

*Helpful hint: A chalkboard can be personalized, too, by painting designs in the corners.

- Brush a thin coat of your favorite color (water-based house paint) over the corkboard. Let it dry and give it one more light coat. Be careful that you're not too goopy with the paint. Brush it on evenly and lightly — that way, your corkboard will stay "corky."

- Leave the middle part bare, and stencil around the edges to create a border for your board.

- Pushpin some photos or magazine cutouts in an artistic pattern.

All Hands on Deck

If you go nuts for anything nautical, you can actually batten down the hatches in your own room by familiarizing yourself with a few sailor's secrets. Using materials that are found on any sea-bound voyage can make your room feel like the hull of a ship. Scott and the girls looked at pictures of boats and ships and got some big ideas for Nat's room.

Here are a few basic things you can do:

1. Try wrapping rope around your bedposts. Learn how to tie a basic nautical knot and tie your rope off at the ends to give your bed the look and feel of a ship's deck.
2. Fishnet can be hung on a wall or draped around your mirror. If there's a tackle box handy, take those flies out of the box and hang them on the wall with tacks or nails, or in a display case.
3. If you live by the ocean, an old buoy that washes up on the beach can be hung on a closet doorknob or on your bedpost. Or you can copy Scott and the girls and just paint the shape of a buoy on a bookshelf. Nicki said it was the easiest thing she did.

The Post-Game Report

What happens after a few weeks go by? Does the excitement of a newly redone room lose its luster for the *Trading Spaces* boys and girls? Not exactly. We checked in with Nat and Nicki, who gave us a full report.

THE FRIENDS . . .

Nat says that when his friends — or even friends of his three siblings — come over, his room is the first stop. One of Nat's buds, also a history buff, was even more blown away than Nat expected. "I explained it slightly to him, but it was a lot more dramatic than I explained."

Nicki's had her share of visitors as well: "I've had lots of people come over and they're just stunned. They think it's pretty cool."

AND FAMILY . . .

Now, Nicki's sister visits her room "a lot." Her sister also has plans of her own: She's redoing her room in an underwater theme, according to Nicki. "I'm redoing my bathroom," adds Nicki, "to go with my room, too." Sounds like a pretty busy household.

Nat's little sister had a different reaction: The skull and crossbones, placed just where she could spy them from her room, really scared her at first. Now she's gotten used to the flag, but that might be something for you to keep in mind if you're crazy for all things pirate — paint the skull and crossbones where no little sibs will be spooked.

THE HOST WITH THE MOST— Diane !

> "I talk to the kids, and they just give me so much energy. I get to act like a big kid. . . . I know it sounds kinda dorky, but that's just who I am!"
> — Diane

Diane

FULL NAME: Diane Mizota

WHAT SHE DOES ON *Trading Spaces: Boys vs. Girls*

Diane is the host of *Trading Spaces: Boys vs. Girls*, which means that she has tons of tasks. Not only does she make sure that the designers and kids are on track, narrate the show, and hang out with the families, but she also helps both designers paint, sew, and put things together!

BACK IN THE DAY

When Diane was a kid, her room lacked style — big-time. "I was really kinda geeky . . . and I never had paint on my walls." But she always had a wild imagination, even if it didn't surface in her room. "I'm constantly bugging Scott and Jordin to put my childhood fantasies into their rooms."

TRAINING

After going to school for communications, acting, and dance, Diane is well qualified to keep time on the *Trading Spaces* set. And she's comfortable in front of the camera, since she's performed in everything from Gap commercials to television shows. Staying cool under pressure is part of what makes Diane an awesome host — plus, she's always ready to spring into action! "I try to help out when there's something fun and creative. . . . I love doing little projects, and I always have."

IDEAS YOU CAN USE

"The biggest and most inexpensive, easiest change to make is paint. A bold paint choice changes the feel of the room completely . . . it's totally inexpensive. And if you hate it, it's easy to change back, paint over. It's not permanent."

ADVICE

Diane is big on creating a room that reflects the person who lives there. "Kids need to find what they feel comfortable in." The only way to do that is to try different things! "You can make bold choices, and they work." The key is taking your interests, your passions, and making the room personal to *you*.

Haley

Haley, age 10, loves horses and hanging with her friends.

The big basement should have been the perfect place for Haley to have friends over, but it lacked some serious personality. Luckily, Matt and Dan wanted to change all that!

Brittany

Brittany, Matt's sister, was ready to step up to the plate, giving Haley a hand with Matt's room.

HORSE HEAVEN

Have you moved forward at a full gallop, while your room is dragging slowly behind? Are you chomping at the bit for some change? Haley was looking to make the most out of her giant playroom, while keeping the horse theme a "stable" influence. Matt and his best buddy Dan are willing to jump in the saddle to turn Haley's room around.

A DAY AT THE RACES

"I think Haley's dream room would be horses, because that's her main passion." — Matt

BASEBALL FIELD

Do you have your own field of dreams? Matt did. He dreamed of a change-up that would put him in the strike zone around the clock. But to get his room done right, Matt needed an assist from friend Haley and sister Brittany.

THE MAJOR LEAGUES

"We just sit there in the stadium seats and watch a baseball game; it's pretty cool. It feels like you're in the stadium because of the wallpaper mural." — Matt

Whose room is this?

Matt

Matt, age 13, is a big-time baseball fanatic.

He thought his room "was *pretty* cool the way it was before," but then the redo scored major points with him!

Dan

Matt recruited Dan to help turn Haley's room into a place fit for her — and her favorite creatures.

HALEY'S CRIB RE-CREATED!

Haley confessed that even though her playroom is the biggest room in the house, none of the furniture matches. "Since it was the basement, we'd put all the old furniture in it." The size and scope of this playroom give it potential, but no one's taken the time to add any character. Haley and her sister aren't so into their limited storage options, either. Dan's right when he says Haley's horses need a new home. Luckily, Jordin and the guys are galloping to the rescue.

At the Starting GATE

BEFORE

This catch-all isn't quite cutting it.

A nice try, but it's time for some cleaner laundry.

A Shetland-sized table is too tiny for Haley and sis.

"I want my room redone because there's not enough storage." — Haley

The Inside Track

From ages 6 to 11, Jordin slept in a bed her dad constructed. It had a built-in closet as a headboard and bookshelves as a footboard. A piece of plywood connected the closet headboard to the bookshelf footboard and Jordin says that made it extra special because "...it felt like a false ceiling." She gets all dreamy when she thinks of it. "I loved this bed! It felt so cool to be in it, like it was a room within a room."

Jordin dressed for the occasion.

Back in the SADDLE

Haley's love of horses is taken to equestrian extremes in her newly perfected playroom. No matter where Haley hangs her riding hat, coming back to this room is guaranteed to make her smile. And everyone else in the family agrees. "I know my mom's favorite thing is the stalls and the horses in them," Haley says. "They made it really personal." Giddyap!

A Photo Finish

Like most horse fanatics, Haley had some favorite friends. So, Jordin and the boys found out which horses were Haley's most beloved, took their pictures, and enlarged them. Then they pasted the life-size images on the inside of Haley's new barn doors.

Why not pin up a picture that's important to you? Most copy shops will make photo enlargements and oversized laser prints. You can even get posters! Blowing up photographs you love can personalize your room.

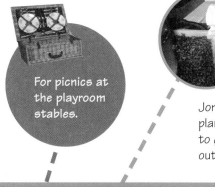

For picnics at the playroom stables.

Jordin and the guys planted plastic hedges to give the room a real outdoorsy feeling.

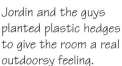

AFTER

The Real Deal: Saddle 'em Up!

A horse is a horse, of course. But is all riding the same? Not exactly. There are two main types of saddled riding: Western (like the kind we associate with cowboys) and English (imagine a fancy riding jacket and slim pants). A Western saddle is bigger and more comfortable — perfect for galloping over rough terrain. An English saddle is smaller, allowing for closer contact with the horse — perfect for graceful strides and jumps. Which do you prefer? The English manner or the Wild, Wild West?

MATT'S DIGS REDONE!

Matt's love of baseball goes way beyond center field, so his old bedroom had three strikes against it. Before Scott and the girls took over, Matt says, "I had a bed, just a normal bed, and I had a desk that I did homework at, and shelves. It was the average room." Matt tried to infuse his digs with a baseball spirit, but the result was cluttered.

In the Know

When it was all done, we asked Matt what advice he'd give to other kids thinking about redoing their rooms. "Try to match it to your personality," he said, "because I think you'll always be happier like that." Sounds like a good idea. And Matt does look a lot happier himself.

Bases EMPTY

BEFORE

Matt's room has been the same "for about seven years."

Matt's had it with the hat pile.

Sorry, Mom and Dad...wrong sport.

"My dream room would be sort of a stadium setup. Baseball is my favorite sport to play." — Matt

Time to organize! The Batter's Box

Is storing your sports gear starting to clutter your clubhouse? Bins and boxes are easy to find and easy to use. They come in all sizes, shapes, and colors. What's your preference — wood, plastic, metal, cardboard? Stack 'em, line 'em up, or put 'em on a shelf like Scott did. Practical and pretty cool-looking, too!

LINE Drive

For a boy who is at his best in the ball-park, this is a field of dreams come true! Matt's new room puts him right inside the baselines — literally. From his infield position he can almost hear the roar of the crowd.

"Dan wanted to stay in there forever, because there was a Game 1 Philly's helmet; that was pretty cool."
— Matt

AFTER

Get your popcorn and peanuts here!

Matt keeps his eye on the ball — even when he's sleeping in his brand-new circular bed.

A dugout desk built for a cleanup hitter.

Peel, Paint & Ponder

Sharing Your Space

Got any brothers or sisters? Chances are if there's a sibling in the house, you know the perils and pleasures of sharing space. Whether it's a bedroom or a playroom, sharing may be important, but it can also be tricky. Divide and conquer the sticky situation by creating a room within a room. Are you flying solo? Don't turn the page too quickly. It's also important for an only child to learn to divide.

Jordin and the guys understand the power of division. Haley's superbig room is broken up by this hedge.

This baseball-card curtain would make a home run of a room divider, too.

All Right...Break It Up!

Even if you don't share a room with a sib, you might want to divide your room for your own uses. The first step is to make a list of your in-pad activities: reading, writing, singing, playing.... Then survey your space: Is there a place to do all those things? Circle the things that need a better spot. Now you're ready to create that separate space.

Here are some ideas:

- **Bookends.** Bookshelves can be moved away from the wall and used as a divider.
- **I Screen, You Screen.** For not a lot of cash, you can buy a standing foldout screen, either plain or with a pattern. A simple screen divides space neatly and cleanly.
- **Curtain Time.** You can divvy up your digs with a curtain. All you need is some fabric. Staple-gun it to your ceiling or drape it from a curtain rod and some eyehooks.
- **Window of Opportunity.** Use a window (hand-crafted or bought from a hardware store) to separate with see-through style. Ask an adult to help you dangle the window frame from the ceiling.
- **Separate Colors.** Painting one wall a different color helps to give that part of your room a different feel.
- **Throw It Down!** Laying a throw rug in a corner of your room could mark it off as a separate section — the "music area" or the "reading room," for example.

Craft, Create & Construct

Now that your space is well defined, start thinking about some of the finer points —
the details.

Fly Ball

Scott and the girls came up with wild and wacky lamps for Matt's ceiling. If you want to shed more light on your love of baseball, but this idea seems too complicated, try something simple. Remove the fixture from your ceiling light. Buy a "globe" fixture (round ball), in a frosted white. Using red acrylic paint and a tiny, narrow brush, paint the stitches of a baseball on it. Let it dry and attach it to the fitting around your light. Heads up! It's a fly ball!

Batter Up

Do you have a wooden bat that brings you better luck in the corner of your room than in the batting cage? Don't let that bat sit idly by. Put it to work with this neat idea for a hat rack:

1. Draw a straight, even line from the handle to the bottom of your bat.
2. With a marker, draw four equally spaced dots along the straight line.
3. Screw a small-to-medium-sized hook into each dot mark.
4. On the other side of the bat, attach two picture hooks 1 to 2 inches in from either end of the bat.
5. Get an adult's advice on how to hang your new hat-rack bat on the wall or on the back of your door.

Off the Mound

Is your baseball card collection growing faster than you can file them? Haley and Brittany made window shades out of protective sheets and color copies of Matt's cards. That's one thing you can do to put your favorite cards to use.

Here's another:
1. Measure the length and width of the top of your desk. Drag an adult to a hardware store or a glass shop to get a piece of glass cut to match the size of your desktop.
2. On one side of the glass, place thin cork or rubber stoppers on each of the four corners.
3. Place your baseball cards on the surface of your desk and secure them with tiny pieces of tape. You can cover your entire desk with them or put down only a few.
4. Gently and carefully place the glass over your desktop and you'll have the whole lineup ready to play ball!

Megan

Megan, age 13, is crazy for South Beach and dreams of being a designer someday.

For four years, Megan has had the same decor. She is looking for a little more inspiration. A lover of art deco architecture, Megan feels right at home in her sizzling new abode.

Christina

To inspire a new look for Justin's crib, Megan has teamed up with her friend Christina. Together they have the power to make serious waves for Justin.

Chapter 7

MIAMI HEAT

Do the beautiful beaches of Florida send you into flights of fancy? Does the moonlight in Miami put you in the best mood? Megan's obsession with sandy beaches and board-walk strolls started with her family vacations in South Beach. Ever since, she's been seeing her babyish bedroom as having a cloudy overcast. Justin and his twin brother, Ryan, enlisted Scott to help them in a complete overhaul of Megan's under-the-weather digs.

LIFE'S A BEACH!

"It's a totally different room.... It feels fun."
— Megan

SURF SHACK

Are you endlessly waiting for high tide in a low-tide room? Justin's an exciting guy with colorful tastes, but his bedroom was a big bummer. He was surfing for something splashier, so Megan and her friend Christina teamed up with Jordin to turn the tide in Justin's room.

ENDLESS SUMMER

"My worst nightmare of a room would have to be black walls or black carpet." — Justin

Whose room is this?

Justin

Justin, age 14, loves the beach and can't wait to catch the next wave.

Justin is a vibrant, colorful guy — his friends think of him as "outgoing." Sadly, his old room did not have the same sunshiny glow. His new Surf Shack is a definite improvement.

Ryan

To improve Megan's room, too, Justin didn't have to look very far for a partner. He chose his twin brother, Ryan.

MEGAN'S CRIB RE-CREATED!

Megan has clearly outgrown her rock-a-bye-baby bedroom. She's ready for a grown-up upgrade. No more pale pink walls and fluffy dust ruffles adorning her bed. Scott and the boys are on their mark and ready to hit the boardwalk for some signs of Megan's favorites . . . South Beach style.

In the Know

What do you love most about your new room?
"Everything! They put blow-up pictures in front of my windows and the sun comes through them in the morning, so I really like that."
— Megan

Rock-a-BYE, baby

BEFORE

This doll collection is sweet, but does it deserve its own shelf?

The pink-and-purple look isn't exactly sizzling.

This solo rocking chair is traded for more social seating.

"Megan's room is really, really big and kind of babyish, like pink and girly."
— Justin

On the Boards

Why settle for a regular headboard? The guys didn't! Scott, Barte, Justin, and Ryan attached a fully constructed hotel front to personalize Megan's headboard in the coolest way. Why not personalize your headboard, too? Paint it, bead it, add a string of lights — just remember to leave room to rest your head!

Moon over MIAMI

What is Megan's obsession with South Beach all about? Justin says, for one thing, "She likes all the architecture." Scott, Justin, and Ryan used Barte's expertise as a masterful builder to bring Megan these mini versions of her favorite structural style. Hand-painted hotel signs — from real places Megan knows and loves — give it a personal touch with authenticity.

Host Diane is pretty impressed: "This isn't really a room. It's more of an environment."

AFTER

Back in the Day: Art Deco

Back in the days of the roaring twenties and the thrilling thirties, art deco was all the rage. It was a design style that dominated everything from architecture and furniture to advertising and fine art. It was called Modernistic or Style Moderne and didn't receive the name art deco until a British art critic and historian renamed it in the sixties. Art deco was all about being modern, moving forward with the advancements in technology — electric power, telephones, automobiles, and airplanes. The world was growing rapidly and art deco design helped to pick up the pace.

"The Megan" hotel: A place for Megan to rest her head.

Nothing punches up the South Beach vibe better than a palm tree.

An intimate spot for a heart-to-heart with friends.

JUSTIN'S DIGS REDONE!

OK. Justin is fun. He's outgoing. He likes the beach. He's a good-time kind of guy. So why is his room so...blah? Time for a major overhaul and color infusion. Are Megan and Christina up to the task? You bet! They've got some great ideas to make Justin's room just beachy.

Wipeout!

Maybe a better word here would be *washout*. What's up with the character-free room? Justin says it hadn't been redone for, well, quite a while. "I had furniture from when I was two. It was very dull. There wasn't anything to look at." Yes, it is high time for a major revamp. After all, the only swirl of color is his body board, sitting against the wall. Jordin used that as a jumping-off point for her design.

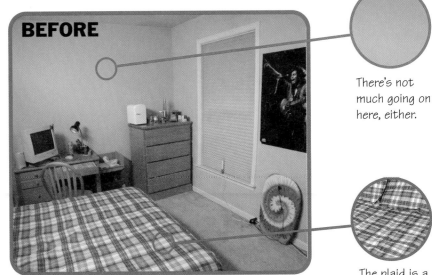

BEFORE

There's not much going on here, either.

The plaid is a good start, but even more color is needed!

"Justin's room does not reflect his personality at all. He's, like, outgoing."
— Megan

Diane helps the girls shed a little sunshine on Justin's walls.

70

All Surf, No Bored

Justin is now surfing the scenes of perpetual summer in the beachiest of bedrooms. "Every time I walk in, it feels like I'm walking in for the first time," Justin raves.

"I get shocked. It's very neat." Surfing is a solo sport, but thanks to Jordin and the girls, Justin's got plenty of room to entertain his friends with his beachfront sofa unit.

For catching a few Zzz's or hanging out with fellow surfer dudes.

AFTER

Justin's body-board shelves bring new meaning to the term "channel surfing."

A touch of tiki.

Back in the Day: The Long and Short of It

No one knows for sure who the first surfer was, but more than one Polynesian seafarer was spotted "riding the waves" for fun in canoes in the late 1700s. The sport took hold in ancient Hawaii, where surfers rode everything from the *paipo*, a two-foot board (used by children, mostly), to the much bigger *olo*, a board reserved strictly for royalty. Wooden-board riding continued for centuries until the 1950s and '60s, when surf equipment did a major 180. Suddenly, surfing was taken to extreme limits, with all the thrills and spills it has today.

How Did They Think of That?

Everyone loves vacations. So why not create your own personal vacation spot to chill in 365 days a year? That's exactly what Megan and Christina were thinking Justin would like. And did they call it correctly? You bet! Justin loves his new beachfront property.

You can also incorporate your favorite vacation spot into your room redo. What's your scene? The beach, the boardwalk, a ski slope, a campsite? Think about the places you love best and consider re-creating them right in your room!

Peel, Paint & Ponder

Just because the seasons change doesn't mean you have to leave them behind for the rest of the year. You can incorporate elements of your favorite season into the landscape of your room, just as Justin and Megan did.

'Tis the Season

Winter
If you dream of snowy mountaintops, you can make a wall mural with white, blue, and gray felt. Cut the felt to create layers of snow on tall mountain cliffs and glue the shapes together for a three-dimensional effect.

Spring
Adopt a tree. You don't need a climate change to bring in a little greenery. You could even use artificial trees made out of plastic or silk. (No need to water!)

Summer
Hit the beach — but for once it's OK to forget the sunscreen. On your wall (or on some poster board) paint a beach scene with a warm sunset right over the water. Instant summer moods are guaranteed!

Fall
Pining for pinecones or fallen autumn leaves? Collect them and make an arrangement in your room. Add splashes of color with orange, red, and yellow leaves.

Aloha, Appliqué

Using appliqué (a French word meaning "to apply"), Jordin and the girls attached the Hawaiian word for "hello" on Justin's curtains to give him an island welcome. Appliqué is a technique that involves ironing and sewing one piece of fabric to another. If you have cloth curtains, you can dress them up this way.

1. Before you do anything, remove your curtains and lay them flat.

2. Choose a piece of fabric you like. Cut out the shapes or words you want to apply.

3. Buy an appliqué kit. This can be found at most sewing or craft stores. Follow the directions on the kit for cutting out the fusible web (the part that makes it all "stick") and ironing on your fabric cutouts.

4. Sew your fabric shapes and words onto your curtain with a sewing machine or by hand. Follow the kit's instructions for finishing it off.

5. Hang those handmade curtains high and be proud of your work.

Dressing It Up with Decoupage

Don't be troubled by an unexciting table, desk, or toy chest. You can amp up their look by adding your own touch, decoupage-style. Use newspaper clippings, color copies of your favorite photos, bits of poetry or song lyrics, even fabric. You can personalize just about anything with decoupage — a desk, trunk, closet door, picture frame, or lampshade.

Here's how:

1. At a craft store, invest in some decoupage glue. (It's usually inexpensive.)
2. Make sure your decoupage surface is free of dust and dirt.
3. With a disposable brush, put a light coat of decoupage glue on the back of your picture. Place your picture down where you want it. Repeat with the other pics — and feel free to overlap!
   Hint: If you have a large surface, work in sections.
   Hint #2: If you're using paper, paste it flat or crinkle it to create an antique look.
4. Let the glue on the back of your pictures dry completely.
5. Now you're ready to decoupage. Put a thin layer of glue over the top (yes, the top) of your design.
6. Let it dry completely and be dazzled by your decoupage design!

Jordin and the girls decoupaged a surfboard and made it into a coffee table for Justin and his friends to gather around.

Stamp It Out

If you have plain, patternless curtains and sewing stupefies you, try using rubber stamps to apply a design. Rubber stamps come in every conceivable pattern and character. Use a stamp in the shape of a fallen leaf for an autumnal look, or your favorite cartoon character for something fun. Just spread your curtain out on a flat surface and dip your stamp in fabric paint. Press the stamp into the fabric and pull it away quickly. Keep going and stamp your way to cooler and more creative-looking curtains.

"Kids have a lot more imagination [than adults do]. They don't see limitations. They always want to do more, more, and more. Adults don't have that imagination. They can't quite imagine taking a surfboard and turning it into a coffee table."
— Jordin

73

Whose room
is this?

Rachael

Rachael, age 10, already knows what she wants to be when she grows up. That's because she's already doing it: singing, acting, and performing. But her room had no star quality. It's up to her friend Evan to add pizzazz.

Marissa

Rachael's friend Marissa was on hand to help trade those spaces. Marissa's laid-back attitude was a big help at crunch time!

BROADWAY BABE

There was nothing wrong with Rachael's old room. There was nothing super spectacular about it, either. It had belonged to the girl who lived there before Rachael's family moved in. Its faded vibe might have worked for that girl, but not for Rachael, a sunny, zesty, bursting-with-talent 10-year-old who lives, breathes, and belts out songs like the budding Broadway star she is. Team *Trading Spaces* moved in and — applause, applause! — the new room sparkles!

RACHAEL CITY MUSIC HALL

"Purple is my favorite color."
— Rachael

ROCK & ROLL RULES

Evan's old room worked for the sports-lovin' karate kid he used to be — his martial arts trophies lined the walls. Lately, he's into rock groups and his drum lessons. And what about the color blue? Bor-ing! Designer Scott brought the passion and the know-how the girls' team needed. The rockin' redo included red walls sponged with black to make a snakeskin effect, a performance stage, killer amps . . . and a black ceiling. Awesome!

ROCKIN' EVAN'S WORLD

"I think it's really gonna look like a rock show in here." — Scott

Evan

Like lots of boys, Evan, age 11, was all about sports: His favorite was karate. Like lots of boys' rooms, Evan's was blue. As in, carpet, bedspread — all of it.

Today, music rocks his world — the louder, the better! Could his friend Rachael and her buddy Marissa play that tune?

Dylan

As for Rachael's room redo, Evan knew he'd need a good friend to share the spotlight. Enter Dylan.

RACHAEL'S CRIB RE-CREATED!

Making the transformation from this cute little girl's room to one that really sparkled and said "Rachael City Music Hall" was a job for Evan, his friend Dylan...and the star of many a show herself, Jordin!

What's WRONG with This Picture?

The carpet was rose-petal pink. The walls — all four — were pale green. The bed's white wooden headboard abutted the far wall, a collection of stuffed animals perched on the shelf above the bed. About the only way you could tell anything about the girl who lived there was a stack of *Playbill* magazines, one for each Broadway show she'd seen. Oh, yes, and a collection of Broadway snow globes.

BEFORE

This flowery valance is too princessy for a Broadway babe.

A hint of a star-to-be.

"I didn't like the flowery thing hanging down over the window. Yuck!"
— Rachael

Time to Organize!

Beneath the stage, Ginene installed storage bins: lots of space for all of Rachael's stuff! More drawers are underneath her bed.

PAINTING THE TOWN . . . PURPLE?

Draped in a slinky, sparkly, going-to-the-theater dress, Jordin put the soundtrack from *Chicago* in the CD player and visualized getting Rachael's room from drab to fab — in 48 frenzied hours. So, first? The walls had to come down. OK, not down, more like done up, down, and all around. The team painted a New York cityscape mural covering three walls. Outlines of New York's famous buildings and neighborhoods were silhouetted against shimmering shades of purples, lilac, and lavender.

What's RIGHT with This Picture?

All That Jazz. Put your hands together and give it up for Rachael City Music Hall — her *Trading Spaces* room has style and pizzazz.

It's a place Rachael can perform, work, dream — and ALL...THAT...JAAAAZZZ!

But not just "any" star! Jordin snagged this prop from the world's most famous department store — it used to serve as the stylized apostrophe on the front of NYC's Macy*s.

AFTER

The Best Seats in the House

Every great performance needs an audience. Evan and Dylan helped move Rachael's bed away from the wall, so it faced the front of the stage — and swapped out her old headboard for a new, extremely cool sideboard. From the back, the sideboard looks like theater seats. And, nice touch, the damask fabric is the same as they used in the curtains. When Rachael's not on stage, she's sitting (or sleeping) in the front row!

The Chrysler Building library.

The mirrored chandelier (and a spotlight or two) light up this Broadway theater.

Any theater worth its New York rep has box seats — and so does Rachael's. But the box seats Jordin dreamed up hide two important and practical pieces of furniture. The illusion of the box seat on stage left (see photo, page 74) is really Rachael's desk. And the one on stage right (above) is her mini piano.

77

EVAN'S DIGS REDONE!

Evan's childhood bedroom was all about an active, sports-lovin' karate kid — see those trophies? It was an average room for a typical young boy. Bed propped against the wall, blue carpet, toys, stuffed animals, Rollerblading equipment. It ALL went buh-bye! Here's what came in — and how they did it!

What's WRONG with This Picture?

First up for the team was a new hue — bye-bye, baby blue, hello, rockin' red and blazing black!

Evan had originally hoped for an all-black room, but Scott and the girls created an even cooler feeling. The walls were painted an eye-popping shade of red, then sponged with black, a technique called Scumbling. Topped with a black ceiling, it gave Evan's room a real rock-and-roll vibe.

BEFORE

Phew! That's a lot of awards!

This drum needs a more rockin' locale.

"I didn't like anything in my old room."
— Evan

CHECKMATE

Time for a new floor, mate! Rachael knew that Evan's old floor had to go: "Since he likes chess, we thought we'd make the floor tiles a chessboard." Using plain old everyday black-and-white vinyl tiles, the team created a life-size board. But what's a chessboard without chess pieces? Scott goes online for everything over-size — like these chess pieces that Rachael and Marissa clearly approve of!

What's RIGHT with This Picture?

Pretty much everything! It's a radical redo and raging rock-and-roll success!

Hide-a-Bed: Evan's stage was constructed with rollers underneath — the perfect place for his bed. To sleep, he just pulls it out. And when bedroom morphs to rehearsal space, he can slide the bed back under!

Rock, Roll & Rehearse!

Real rockers need real stages to rehearse and to rock out on! Evan got his, thanks to the *Trading Spaces* trio of Scott, Rachael, and Marissa, who dreamed it, and carpenter Barte, who constructed it. The wooden stage goes wall-to-wall under the window. In front of and above the stage, the team constructed a steel tressel — to hold those spotlights, of course!

Flickerfest

Rockers need paloozas, right? Summer concert fests are awesome. And lucky Evan has his very own Flickerfest! Flanking his stage are flickerdot boards! They're huge, 6 feet by 4 feet! Flickerdot boards are used as billboards, and they sort of sway in the breeze and reflect light.

Barte asks, "Is it level?" And Marissa gives a resounding "Yep!"

Study, Buddy

Evan's desk was created using a large tabletop held up by a wooden 2 x 4 and some chains (very rock and roll!) instead of legs. Above and around are plastic shelves to hold all his stuff. Other storage areas were constructed beneath the stage, on either side of Evan's hideaway bed, and in his double-door closet.

Peel, Paint & Ponder

Making Rachael's Room a Reality

Not everyone can dream the redo as Jordin did, but most everyone can re-create it — or do it à la carte: Take the parts you like. Here's how:

Unique and Useful

Rachael's new room is fit for the star she will someday be, but it also works for the fifth grader she is now. "Form will meet function here," says Jordin as Evan and Dylan bring in wrought-iron shelves to house Rachael's books, snow globe collection, CDs — even her ballet slippers.

The shelving units were topped off with wooden replicas of famous New York City buildings, including the tiered-top Chrysler Building and slanted Citicorp Building.

Think Inside the Box!

Evan, Dylan, and the *Trading Spaces* crew made Rachael her very own New York City skyline. It looks superimpressive, and it's supereasy for you to re-create at home.

Here's how:

1. Collect boxes. Lots of them. You can use shoe boxes, cereal boxes, even jewelry boxes, or egg cartons for smaller decorations.
2. Tape the boxes together with packing tape in whatever shape you want. You could make a cityscape, or try something different — a robot, a dinosaur, an Olympic platform....
3. Measure and cut paper to cover your boxy figure.
4. Paint your creation with bright, vivid colors.

Remember to use your imagination — don't box yourself in!

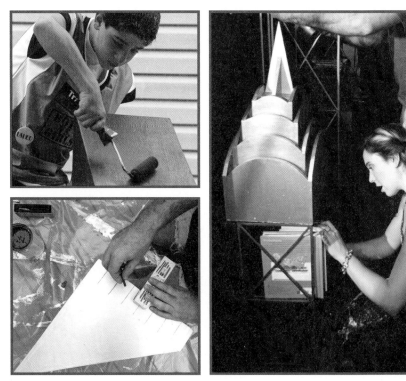

Craft, Create & Construct

Making Evan's Room Your Reality

Dance Floor Stage

The stage in Evan's room was created by carpenters, but what's that shiny black stuff covering it, and how can you get that effect? It's a special laminate flooring that comes in either black or white. It's high-gloss shiny and used on dance floors. Typically sold in 4-foot-by-8-foot square sheets, it runs about $40. Bonus: It sweeps up easily!

Going Dotty

Like the flickerdot billboard in Evan's room? You, too, can snag 'em. They look like mirrored sequins and come in strips — 14 dots on each thin (one-inch-wide) strip. They're applied with hot glue guns.

Making an entire billboard — or two! — out of these flickerdot strips was, to say the least, very labor intense. Everyone on the team, including Diane, pitched in. It was like arts and crafts period at camp!

Safety Tip #5: Pay Attention to the Buzz

Have you seen someone operate machinery — heard the buzz of a table saw, the hum of a sander, or the whirr of a power drill — and thought, *Yeah, I wanna do that*? Well, consider yourself warned: It looks a lot easier than it is! Even people who use power tools professionally need to pay complete attention to what they're doing. Keep an eye on the people you're working with and make sure that everyone stays alert — sometimes even adults need supervision when using dangerous tools! Always feel free to correct them if they're losing their focus. Everyone will be safer for it.

81

Meet Ginene, Carpenter Queen!

"There are crazy things that only your imagination can come up with, that you can physically make and do." — Ginene

FULL NAME: Ginene Licata

WHAT SHE DOES ON *Trading Spaces: Boys vs. Girls*
As a main character on the show, Ginene's turned fantasy into living reality. She's transformed a regular room into a half basketball court, and the typical den of an aspiring actress into a private screening room. Not to mention building that awesome pirate ship deck in Nat's captain's quarters.

BACK IN THE DAY
Ginene was born with the woodworking gene.
"I was always Dad's helper. We have pictures of when I was three, handing him bricks when he's building the fireplace. We built a couple of decks onto houses. We refinished some basements and made built-in cabinets." All this led Ginene to a double major of technical theater and acting in college.

HER OWN ROOM REDO
At 13, she decided that her former obsessions, the color purple and unicorns, were so yesterday. She rearranged all the furniture, took a blue bedspread from another room, and — with Mom's approval —sponge-painted the ceiling and created an outrageous mural on the wall.

NAILIN' IT: IDEAS YOU CAN USE
When working on her own room, Ginene came up with low-tech ideas anyone can use. She painted the molding around the walls and doors all different colors. She made a set of "worry" dolls and glued them to the top of the molding above her closet door.

ADVICE
"Your room is ultimately your own private expression, for yourself. Anything is possible. Don't be afraid of your decisions, your choices, or your creative ideas."

IT STARTS WITH Barte!

"I've always been interested in design and creating things." — Barte

FULL NAME: Barte Shadlow

WHAT HE DOES ON *Trading Spaces: Boys vs. Girls*

Like Ginene, Barte works alongside the *TS* designers, helping to bring the kids' visions to reality. He's the go-to woodworking dude who — for instance — crafted the stage for the rock-and-roll room, and the hotel headboard in Megan's Miami pad.

BACK IN THE DAY

Barte hails from Australia. His family moved quite often, so his memories include many different bedrooms. The weirdest was the garage! "It was a big room, and we set up a tennis [Ping-Pong] table in there. I had my own shower and a little kitchenette." He also had a possum living in the roof! "It just got in somehow. He scratched and gnawed a hole right above where my shower was. I got into my shower one morning and I looked up and there's this gray, furry possum body hanging out of this hole. He was very comfortable."

TRAINING

Barte actually went to university for landscape architecture. So how did the whole carpentry thing happen? Almost by accident: Barte needed a stand for his drawing board, but unfortunately didn't have the money for a store-bought one. "I ended up buying some lumber and making one for myself. It was kind of challenging, but it was also very fulfilling to have something that I made for myself."

ADVICE

"I think a kid needs to have something fun in the room that reflects his or her personality and interests — something that, every time they saw it or used it, would encourage them to pursue their hopes, their dreams."

Kali

Kali, age 13, left childhood behind to kick in her teenage years with a fresh new pad.

Whose room is that?

Eli

Eli, age 11, staked his claim on secondhand digs that needed a dose of boy style.

It's all in the family!

Kali and Eli are brother and sister.

Chapter 9

DOO-WOP DINER

Kali's room redo went big-time retro, with a nod to the teenage days of yesteryear.... Though Kali has both feet firmly planted in the present, she's really into the 1950s. Her new blast-from-the-past room gives her a 3-D view of a hangout spot from her favorite era. She can go solo at the soda counter or let her buddies call for best dibs on a seat in her new diner booth.

SHAKE, RATTLE, AND ROLL!

"This [room] is the coolest thing ever." — Kali

SECRET AGENT TRAINING CAMP

When everyone else in the family mellows out after a long day, are you still ready to climb the walls? Eli is, at least according to his sister Kali, who describes her bro as "really hyper." His old room didn't equate with his energized enthusiasm. Why? It's not classified information: Until recently, the purple-bound pad belonged to his sister.

CLIMBING THE WALLS

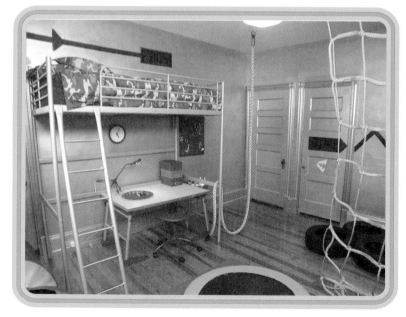

"My friends said it was amazing. My parents started climbing things." — Eli

Kali and Eli were ready to roll with serious sibling rivalry, when two surprise teammates snuck on the scene for some double-agent dueling. Daryl Sabara and Alexa Vega, the stars of *Spy Kids,* intercepted the *Boys vs. Girls* call to action!

The Rules
Since both rooms are in the same house — and since our teams are being helped by a pair of big-time, big-screen spies, Diane sets up strict rules of conduct.

Diane: "There will be no spying on your room."

Alexa Vega: "Oh, come on, that's what we're here for."

Diane: "Yes. And I anticipated that by spy-proofing the house."

85

KALI'S CRIB RE-CREATED!

Kali had just moved into her new crib, and it was looking pretty sparse. Not a whole lot on the walls, some dull gray carpeting... Sweeping changes were in order, so Scott and the boys cooked up some ideas. Kali's room is getting a sassy update for her old-school tastes.

LATER, Alligator!

Kali just left childhood behind, and she wants her digs to follow suit. With a great love of 1950s retro, Kali's tastes hark back to the days of jukeboxes and drive-ins. She's ready to have a blast taking the trip into her teenage years, but her regular room is a real party pooper. Scott and the guys are saying "later" to drab space as they create a fab new place.

BEFORE

Painting, coolsville. Room, a little dullsville.

This patchwork quilt is quaint, but it dates back to the wrong era.

"I just moved into the room down the hall because I wanted more space and I wanted to get away from my brother."
— Kali

A clue about her character: Kali likes to look back and forward.

Daryl: "Eli, do you know what this is?"
Eli: "Uhhh, no."
Daryl: "Neither do I."
(Actually, it's a gadget that locates the support beams behind a wall.)

Looking like a T-Bird right out of Grease, Scott is ready to rock and roll on Kali's room. Looks like he and the boys are planning a top secret strategy....

Chrome-plated PAD

Kali's room was transformed from a kid's world to a teenager's treasure — 1950s style, that is. In a cushy chrome-plated cot, Kali can wake up to the Sha Na Na sounds of her jukebox and twist her way through the day. She's got it made in her new diner digs — open for business 24 hours a day, 7 days a week.

This room really cooks now.

AFTER

May we take your order?

Kali is sleeping on cloud nine in her cruisin' convertible bed.

Back in the Day: The Jukebox

The jukebox was all the rage in the fifties, but it was invented long before the days of rock and roll.

Nickel-in-the-slot phonographs made their debut in the late 1800s. These big record (as in, old-time album!) players sat in public places where folks could put a nickel in the slot and hear tunes by placing their ear to a listening tube! The jukebox of today, with CDs and pumping speaker systems, sure isn't what it used to be.

Let's Hear from You

What is your favorite thing in your room?

"I really like spiritual things. I have lots of candles and a pillow with a moon on it — and a big Sailor Moon poster." — Grace, 12

"I put up little lanterns my aunt sent me. Little rice paper clouds." — Anna, 15

ELI'S DIGS REDONE!

Is your room a hand-me-down, with elements from its last occupant that are not your style at all? Look and learn, friends. Here's how the girls personalized Eli's inherited space.

Consider THIS

What do you do when you inherit a room? Put up a few new pictures, change the furniture around? Sometimes that's just not enough. Eli's hand-me-down digs lack the stamp of his spirited vibe. Never one to go the timid route, Jordin's ready to lead the girls in a major top-to-bottom room revamp. Eli knows he wants "sports" in his room, but he has no idea just how many he's going to get....

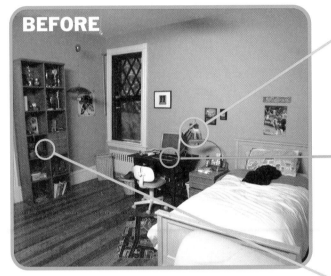

BEFORE

Dusting for fingerprints.

This is no place to keep secret files.

How long has Eli been snooping? The flashlight knows all.

"I want to decorate it. The walls are so purple and it's not me." — Eli

Lofty Intentions

Is your old bed on its way out? Has it sprung its last spring? If you're poised and ready for a new bedtime hideaway, now's your chance to create more space, survey your surroundings, and spy from above.

Consider the loft bed. Loft beds allow for more room within your room. A bed on stilts can give you an extra place to put your desk, your reading area, or a top secret spot for going undercover. Leave the underside of your loft bed open to visitors or enclose it with a curtain to protect your private space.

Jordin's getting some top secret advice from Eli's spying fish.

Consider THAT

Eli, the whirling dervish of energy who loves "sports, all sports," got more than he imagined: a Secret Agent Training Camp complete with a climbing wall, monkey bars, trampoline, and a finish line that leaves him off at a loft bed. It's the perfect place to crash after a long training session. Whew.

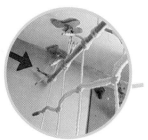

A web of possibilities.

AFTER

TOP SECRET:
AGENT NAME: ELI
ALIAS: Constant Motion

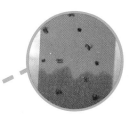

Eli can scale the wall, rock-climbing-style.

Cool tunnel.

The Real Deal: Lingo Language

The spy world has lots of lingo to ensure its activities stay on the down-low. Here are some words that spies have used to keep things on the QT:

Baby-sitter — Someone's bodyguard.
Shoe — A fake passport or traveling visa.
Cover — Refers to a person's alias, their made-up persona.
Ears Only — Something that can be spoken but not written down for someone else to see.
Eyes Only — A document that ya can read, but ya can't discuss.
Chicken Feed — A bit of information. It's not much, but it's a little something to go on.
Spymaster — The top spy — head honcho in a spy operation.

Eli's station of operation, for decoding and detecting.
(Watch out, Kali!)

89

Peel, Paint & Ponder

Jordin and Scott are designers with awesome imaginations. When they match wits with the most daring kids on the block, their choices are anything but ordinary. Take

note: You don't have to follow in the footsteps — or handprints — of others. You can break the mold, make things your own, be weird, be odd, be offbeat. Be yourself.

Anything But Ordinary

For Eli's room, Jordin and the girls donned the walls with silver — Eli's favorite color — and painted an arrow leading the way. Kali's room got a fresh coat of retro fifties turquoise. Neither one of these is your "average" hue. Try using colors that you wouldn't normally associate with wall paint. If metallic silver is your thing and you'd like to unveil a spy vault of your own, we say, GO FOR IT! Instead of asking why, ask why not?

Diane, who felt like her room as a kid was "boring," says working on Trading Spaces: Boys vs. Girls has made her braver: "It shows you that you can make bold choices, and they work. It's not the end of the world if you paint your wall orange, and in fact, it can be really fun."

Sign of the Times

Scott hung a bunch of diner signs in Kali's room that date back to the fifties. You can buy pictures and words from the past in two ways — the originals (sold in antiques stores) or the knockoffs that look exactly like the originals (sold in gift shops). They're easy to find and easy to hang up. A hammer and some nails will do them justice.

Burning Rubber

If you're totally keen on vintage vehicles or modern mobiles, you can bring the chrome home and create a space that fires up your engine.

- Shine up an old hubcap and hang it on your wall.
- A steering wheel can be mounted on the wall over your bed.
- Get with the "greasers" of the 1950s (the biggest fans of cool coupes) and mount a side-view or rearview mirror to the top of your dresser or door molding. Pin up that ponytail in style.
- Collect license plates from times past and present. Create a road map of all 50 states by displaying them on your wall. It might take a while to track down the plates of every state, but the challenge is half the fun of collecting cool things.

Vertical Views

Is your space too small for spreadin' out? Is your horizontal only half of what it should be? Well, things are lookin' up. You can hit the heights of your room by using the vertical space.

Jordin, who grew up in New York City, where the rooms can be tiny but the ceilings can be tall, agrees: "You can always go up, if you don't have the floor space. You have to start thinking vertically instead of horizontally. Use your imagination."

Jordin suggests two things:

- For storage, try taking old (antique) suitcases and stacking them.
- Find an old ladder and fix it up to create a top-of-the-line bookcase.

Some other suggestions:

- No place to put your stereo speakers? Put two corner shelves up high near the ceiling and place your speakers on them.
- No room for storing your bicycle? Did you know that some people hang their bicycles on the wall or from the ceiling?

Craft, Create & Construct

Four walls, one floor, and one ceiling... What to do with all that space?

The Shape of Things

Scott, Eli, and Daryl cut crazy shapes out of paper and used them to paint the wall. You can do this, too, with some paper, paint, and a sponge.

1. Draw and cut your shape out of the center of a piece of paper. Brown newspaper or construction paper is best for this. It's thicker and more durable.
2. Tape the outline of your shape to the wall in the spot you want it.
3. Lightly dip a clean sponge into wall paint. If you need to double-dip, be careful not to overdip. Blot that sponge on a spare piece of paper or cardboard to get rid of any excess paint.
4. Press the sponge into your shape pattern until it's filled with color.
5. Carefully remove your paper pattern to reveal what's underneath.
6. Let it dry and if you dig what you see, you can keep going with it.

The Writing's on the Wall

Jordin, Kali, and Alexa gave Eli's name new meaning by writing it across his wall.

After all, what's in a name? A lot of promise. You can use your name like a secret code, too. Place a letter or two on each wall, one on a door, and so on until you've spelled your name in letters across the room. Have people decode it if they plan on staying for a spell. Have your friends sign their own names on the back of a door.

Hint: You can also write your favorite lines of poetry or the lyrics from a song.

Hand Jive

Perfect your room with your personal imprint. Kali and Alexa decided that Eli's upper wall and ceiling needed a little something special — a dead giveaway that someone had been sneaking around in his space. They left a handprint trail leading from his rock-climbing wall onto his ceiling. But how can a person possibly crawl along the wall or on the ceiling? It's simple. Grab a ladder!

1. Pour a small amount of water-based wall paint into a paint tray or disposable baking pan.
2. Place just the palm of your hand onto the surface of the wet paint. Make sure your palm is flat when you dip, then lift your palm and let it drip. (If you're up to your elbow, you've gone way too far!)
3. Gently place your hand where you want your print to go. Repeat and let your hands do the walking.

Floor It

Scott had big plans for the wood floors under Kali's bedroom rug. But when he and the boys pulled the rug up to reveal the floor underneath, they didn't like what they saw. They made a change in the plan by painting Kali's floor white instead.

Is your floor lacking in style? Consider painting it. This move is guaranteed to change your scenery. And you can be inventive with it. For example...

- If you're into cars, you can lay down tire tracks by taking an old tire and rolling it lightly in paint. Then roll the rubber across your floor for a hot-rod trail.
- Lay down some footprints with an old pair of sneakers. Slip the shoes on your hands, dip lightly, and walk backward. Make a trail from your door to the closet or under your bed. Let people think someone is hiding there.